D0560478

ARTIE
AND
PINK MARSH

CHICAGO IN FICTION
SAUL BELLOW
ADVISORY EDITOR

ARTIE
AND
PINK MARSH

TWO NOVELS BY GEORGE ADE

DRAWINGS BY JOHN T. MC CUTCHEON

INTRODUCTION BY JAMES T. FARRELL

CHICAGO AND LONDON
THE UNIVERSITY OF CHICAGO PRESS

Artie *(1896) and* Pink Marsh *(1897) were first published by*
Herbert S. Stone & Co., Chicago

THE UNIVERSITY OF CHICAGO PRESS, CHICAGO & LONDON
The University of Toronto Press, Toronto 5, Canada

Introduction © 1963 by The University of Chicago. All rights reserved
Published 1963. Printed in the United States of America

George Ade: Creator of

Artie and *Pink Marsh*

A NEW INTRODUCTION

by James T. Farrell

George Ade remains a writer of the first order. His influence upon the literature of the twentieth century is strong and, unfortunately, not always apparent. He was close to Peter Finley Dunne, whom he knew. As Dunne was a great writer, Ade was next door to greatness, and at moments he too achieved greatness. He should be lasting; he was a masterful short-story writer, surpassing O. Henry. I dislike making these comparisons, lifting up one writer at the expense of another, but here there is reason for my doing what normally I condemn.

O. Henry stirs pity for the struggle there was in his life, but in his writings there is often something that does not ring genuine. Too, there is a carefree twisting of everything into the picturesque. It is all largely verbal, a play on sentiment. The "trick ending," the "snapper" that surprises, cancels sincere feeling and the creation of a sense of realness.

Ade was natural, and his characterizations promptly take on reality. He refuses to trick his situations or trademark his endings. They are as natural as the events reported in the newspaper for which he wrote. He called himself a realist, and he qualifies. He began with people, not situations. His realism was a consequence of his interest in people and the talent he had for making them come alive in what he wrote.

Ade was born in 1866, in Kentland, Indiana, a small town about eighty miles from Chicago. The surrounding area was farmland. Ade, as he grew up, turned out not to possess the qualities that make a farmer; but as a boy he was good listener, and he learned to make more than hay out of what city slickers might consider hayseed talk. Ade listened to endless talk, and he heard dialogue, dialogue about the weather and other subjects that are the common currency of people who have nothing to say to each other. He heard the humor of it. The early Hoosier days were the source of his flavorful language and the originality in its use that became George Ade's contribution to American literature — the use of language "as it is spoke" in his short stories and fables.

He started as a newspaper writer. Day after day he wrote his "Fables in Slang"; and day after day he had fresh subjects, he did not repeat himself. His ironic touches, his alert regard for the twists and turns of fate, his good-natured humor, and — it needs to be said — his sometimes Philistine smugness. Yes, these are some of the traits and qualities found in the writings of George Ade.

He had an ear, an eye, and a ranging curiosity about people and their destinies.

Here are two early volumes by George Ade: *Artie*, which was originally published in 1896, and *Pink Marsh*, first issued in book form in 1897. By that time Ade could consider himself a success. He had attracted the notice, among others, of William Dean Howells and Hamlin Garland. But before he reached Chicago at the age of twenty-four, he graduated from college and tried reading law, and then he got a job as a journalist on a newly founded newspaper in Lafayette, Indiana. The newspaper was *The Call*, and Ade's salary was $8 a week. Next he got a job selling patent medicines for a company that promptly failed. And off he went to Chicago to join his college classmate and lifelong friend, John T. McCutcheon, who was at the station to meet him and took him along to the hall bedroom they were to share. George Ade's half of the rent was to be $2.50, and to afford it he had to have a job. He was promptly hired by the *Morning News*, to do a daily piece on the weather.

To coin a banality, it seemed an inauspicious beginning. And it would have been so for almost anyone but George Ade. He was older than the pluck-and-luck boys of Horatio Alger Jr.'s imagination, but he had something better than a shoeshine box to help him make the most of opportunity. He had George Ade. And George Ade could make even the weather seem interesting.

Soon he began to do general reporting, and his pay was raised to $15 a week. He did legwork, going out on all kinds of stories. He came to know Chicago "like a laboratory." This experience prepared him for the writing he was to do. He saw much more of Chicago than a reporter is likely to see today. He saw it purely and simply. He had lived close to the farm, in a small town. Everywhere there were sharp contrasts to be seen.

In almost all of the earlier writings about Chicago that have retained their significance, the writers had this advantage of perceiving in contrasts. They came to Chicago as to something new. The very coming to Chicago was a story, or a part of a story. It was even more — it was an adventure, a change of life. Chicago was new, a city of many hopes, the locale of adventure. It was new not only to writers and aspiring writers, but to thousands and thousands of people. In a sense, Chicago was new to itself. Dreiser had his own sense of Chicago as new, and he saw the rising inland metropolis as a Venice of dreams. Ade was the greater realist. He was realistic about people and their patterns of behavior, and he was less likely to be upset by their foibles and their blindnesses.

Artie and *Pink Marsh* can be classified as novels. Each consists of a series of episodes taken from Ade's newspaper columns. Ade chose only the best of the pieces about Artie and Pink Marsh and their encounters and experiences in and about Chicago. And from these random pieces we can feel emerge Ade's sense of character.

For the creation of Artie Blanchard he drew literally on a boy who worked in the art department of his newspaper. Ade's biographer, Fred Kelly, quotes the boy:

"I didn't do a thing but push my face in there [a church entertainment] about eight o'clock last night, and I was 'it' from the start. Say, I like that church and if they'll put in a punchin' bag and a plunge, they can have my game, I'll tell you those."

Ade used this verbatim in *Artie*. Most writers do something like this, but first there is invention, the use of the imagination, the creation of character and event in sequence, the establishment of the illusion of reality — even the choice of where and how the verbatim quotations are to be used. Life itself is the model for writers, always — even if it be a pattern of fantasy and dream that violates the laws of the external universe.

Artie works in a business office, not a newspaper office. He goes about as much as he can, and he tells his experiences to Miller, who is older and rather sedate. Miller does not know what the city is like after working hours. In telling his experiences, Artie grows. He falls in love, and we find him love-struck and moony and younger than he thinks himself to be. Here Ade seems to have had just the right amount of restraint. Ade never laughs at Artie or spills over into sentimentality. This is the way it should be in all good and true fiction. Ade does not need to depend upon suspense to maintain interest in his characters. He does not make them toe a story-line. Again, the characters are the story.

Artie is a natural characterization, with no false or forced caricature. There is no easy evasion by exaggeration, no grotesque clichés on the slapstick level. George Ade gives Artie the simplicity of his human proportions, thus making Artie touchingly real.

Pink Marsh is a Negro shoeshine boy, working in a barber shop one flight down. Like Artie, Pink Marsh confides in someone older than himself, in this case the "morning customer," who likes him, is amused by him, and sometimes offers advice and encouragement.

The use of dialect, phonetically rendered, is not practiced much today. There is less need of it now than there was when George Ade wrote *Pink Marsh*. At that time differences in speech and accent stood out in a very pronounced way.

In the 1890's, differences in behavior, dress, manner and manners, were striking. These were the bubbles to be seen on the surface of the American melting pot. Differences in speech quickly aroused the interest of many. Ade, who had listened to farm folk in Indiana, took the same interest in the prototypes of Artie and

Pink Marsh. These were "new voices" to him. He listened and transcribed. This was a new generation of Americans, who saw a Chicago he would not have seen without their eyes. They were not hod-carriers, teamsters, bricklayers, ditchdiggers, and they were not foreigners. They went to work dressed up, and they expected to rise in the world. They had gone to school — at least to grammar school. Living in the big city, they had lost some of their small-town mores. Some were salesmen, able to travel about in the course of their work. They were beginning to think they knew what for the world is round.

They felt their sense of difference from the mass, the great unwashed, as a quality of their own self-esteem. (This is true of both Artie and Pink Marsh, though neither expresses it directly.) They were very conscious of differences. In a city the size of Chicago differences exist.

Ade pleased them by so carefully reproducing the talk of the "darky," the Irishman with his brogue, the expostulating Italian; and, in a number of instances, the hick or rube who was thought to have straw in his ears and was quick to defend the virtues of the farm and prove his own sagacity.

Other factors were involved in the development of interest in slang and the vernacular. It seemed to express the wonder and reality of city life, of so much that was a part of the world. It had no connection with the twice-removed air of the language in books. Many, of course, had no other command of the language as a means of expression. In Chicago, in particular, it was becoming an electrically alive current in city life. It expressed so much that had not been thought or said.

Pink Marsh, as well as *Artie*, needs to be regarded in a certain perspective, and I have suggested some of the factors which ought to be considered in reading these sketches.

The use of phonetic spelling to catch the sound of living speech was a virtual necessity at the time Ade was creating *Pink Marsh*. Speech in the places of work and of commerce, on street corners, in barber shops, in saloons, in offices, and on front stoops was rich in variety and full of the pathos of differences. And George Ade had learned to express them all without drowning the amusing.

At the time Ade was writing this was so common and so wide-spread, manifest daily, that it became an unavoidable element in popular writing. Mark Twain began it, and after him came George Ade and Peter Finley Dunne. Ring Lardner followed; his successor, I suppose, is Salinger. And I've not mentioned Stephen Crane, whose *Maggie, a Girl of the Streets* contains a phonetic rendering of the voluble discourse of uneducated people.

Pink Marsh is also a forerunner. Pink was living before the racial strain in Chicago became menacing. Pink, of course, serves white men. He is not only unusually talkative, unrestrained, and expressive, but he has an inner core of dignity which sets him apart from the caricatures of Octavus Roy Cohen, of a later date. (I have in mind Florian Slappey, Cohen's chief character.)

The significance of dialect and how it is rendered is forgotten today. It was a means of revealing character, background, social roles, and relationships. Of course, when I imply the terms sociological and psychological I am differentiating only for purposes of emphasis. Human beings are not aggregations of categories, classes, facts, data, and types.

George Ade was criticized because he chose to step down into a barber shop and write about the people he found there. But it is wise to suspect that Ade found Pink and his like more interesting than those Pink served.

Pink describes to the "morning customer" the happenings in which he is involved. These occur among the colored population of the South Side, and they include a good number of accounts of Pink's own experiences with the girls he likes and the men who are his rivals. From chapter to chapter, day to day, Pink grows in a kind of rich, comic reality. Unlike Artie, he is sometimes allowed to be the wise fool. There is much shrewdness in Pink's make-up, underneath the ill-education; and in the same way Artie, who is wise beyond his years, is shown to have a core of naïveté. In both Pink and Artie there is much of Ade's own venturing personality. By endowing Pink and Artie with his own characteristics, George Ade saves them from stereotype. Artie is both knowing and tender; Pink is both an "Uncle Tom" and a true-born Yankee.

The gap between Pink and his customers is revealed in dialogue, but always the energy of his impressions keeps him real. Any air of patronization that the reader wishes to read into Ade's characterization of Pink is dispelled beyond doubt by the clear-eyed view Pink has of those who work in the shop or the customers who come there. Pink is shrewd, knowing, and sometimes farcical, but he has a great measure of sympathic charm. He exists as a real person, with many of Ade's traits and characteristics. Ade could not have written about him if this were not so.

George Ade was a phenomenon, an American phenomenon. He was next door to literary greatness. He was recognized and applauded by the many who came after him. He helped to create and condition the audience now clamoring for the works of American writers.

Oscar Wilde said: "To reveal art and conceal the art is the artist's aim." In *Pink Marsh*, the story of a Negro shoeshine boy with whom George Ade obviously identifies, Ade's birthplace, his education, his experience are concealed — he creates a real character named Pink. This is the phenomenon of George Ade. And the same can be said of his championship of Artie, who is so unlike the Hoosier writer who created him.

Both novels are readable today, almost seven decades after they were written. The two books combined here are among the first in George Ade's career. His writing has a lasting brightness about it. I find that I can reread it today without losing any of the enjoyment I had in many different years of the past.

ARTIE

I

One day Mrs. Morton, wife of the city manager, came to the offices and in polite brigandage compelled each man in the room to pay fifty cents for a ticket to the charity entertainment. This entertainment was to be given at a South Side church on the following Wednesday evening. Artie bought a ticket with apparent willingness.

"I do n't want you young men to think that I'm robbing you of this money," said Mrs. Morton. "I want you to come to the entertainment. You 'll enjoy it, really."

"Blanchard can go all right," suggested Miller, with a wink at young Mr. Hall. "He lives within a few blocks of your church."

"Then he must come," said Mrs. Morton decisively. "Won't you, Mr. Blanchard?"

"Sure," replied Artie, blushing deeply.

"Why, Mrs. Morton, he has n't been in a church for three years," said Miller.

"I do n't believe it," and she turned to Artie, who was shaking his fist at Miller. "Now, Mr. Blanchard, I want you to promise me faithfully that you'll come."

"I'll be there all right," said he, smiling feebly.

"Remember, you've promised," and as she went out she shook her finger at him as a final reminder.

"Well, are you going?" asked Miller.

Artie put on his lofty manner and gazed at his office companions with seeming coldness.

"What 's it to you whether I do or not? Did n't you hear what I said to her? Sure I'm goin'. I've got as much right to go out and do the heavy as any o' you pin-heads. If I like their show I'll help 'em out next time — get a couple o' handy boys and put on a six-round go for a finish. Them people never saw anything good."

"I'll bet you do n't go," spoke up young Mr. Hall.

Artie laughed dryly. "You guys must think I'm a quitter, to be scared out by any little old church show," said he.

That was the last said of the charity entertainment until Thursday morning, when Artie, after dusting off his desk, strolled up to Miller and gave him a friendly blow, known to ringside patrons as a "kidney-punch."

"Ouch!" exclaimed Miller.

"Well, I goes," said Artie.

"Where?" asked Miller, who had forgotten.

"Where? Well, that's a good thing. To the church show — the charity graft. I did n't do a thing but push my face in there about eight o'clock last night, and I was 'it' from the start. Say, I like that church, and if they'll put in a punchin'-bag and a plunge they can have my game, I'll tell you those."

"Did you see Mrs. Morton?"

"How's that, boy? Did I see her? Say, she treated me out o' sight. She meets me at the door, puts out the glad hand and says: 'Hang up your lid and come into the game.'"

"I never heard her talk like that," suggested Miller.

"Well, that's what she meant. She's all right, too, and the only wonder to me is how she ever happened to tie herself up to that slob. It's like hitchin' up a four-time winner 'longside of a pelter. He ain't in her class, not for a minute or a part of a minute. What kills me off is how all these dubs make their star winnin's. W'y, out there last night I see the measliest lot o' jays — regular Charley-boys — floatin' around with queens. I wish somebody 'd tell me how they cop 'em out. Do n't it kill you dead to see a swell girl — you know, a regular peach — holdin' on to some freak with side whiskers and thinkin' she's got a good thing? That's right. She thinks he's all right. Anyway, she acts the part. And say, you know Percival, that works over in the bank — little Percy, the perfect lady. There's a guy I've known for five years, and so help me, if he gets on a street-car where I am, I get off and walk. That ain't no lie. I pass him up. I say, 'You 're all right, Percy, and you can take the car to yourself,' and then I duck."

"Was he there?

ARTIE

"The whole thing! That ain't no kid. He was the real papa — the hit o' the piece. One on each arm, see? — and puttin' up the large, juicy con talk. They was beauts too; you could n't beat 'em, not in a thousand years. There they was, holdin' to this wart. Up goes my hands in the air, and I says to myself: 'Percy, you 're all right. I would n't live on the same street with you, but you're all right at that.' But he could n't see me."

"Could n't see you?"

"No, he lost his eyesight. He looked at me, but he was too busy to see me. No, he had on his saucy coat and that touch-me-not necktie, and oh, he was busy. He was n't doin' a thing. I think I'll give the bank a line on Percy. Any man that wears that kind of a necktie had n't ought to handle money. But you ought to seen the two he had. I'd like to know how he does it. I had a notion to go up to one o' the girls and say 'What's the matter? Ain't you ever seen any others?'"

"Did you like the show?" asked Miller.

"It's this way. They liked it, and so" — with a wave of the hand — "let 'em have it. If they put the same turns on at any variety house the people 'd tear down the buildin', tryin' to get their coin back. Mrs. Morton got me a good seat and then backclapped the show a little before it opened up so I did n't expect to be pulled out o' my chair — and I was n't. If I'd been near the door I'd 'a' sneaked early in the game, but, like a farmer, I let her put me way up in front. I saw I was up against it, so I lasted the best way I could. Two or three o' the songs was purty fair, but the woman that trifled with the piano for about a half an hour was very much on the bummy bum. Then there was a guy called an entertainer, that told some o' the gags I used to hear when my brother took me to the old Academy and held me on his lap. But he got 'em goin', just the same. 'Well,' I says to myself, 'what'd a couple o' hot knock-abouts do to this push?' On the dead, I do n't believe any o' them people out there ever saw a good show. It just goes to prove that there's lots of people with stuff that think they know what 's goin' on in town, but they do n't. I ain't got no kick comin,' only it was a yellow show, and I'm waitin' for forty-five cents change."

"I should think you would have got the worth of your money simply by seeing so many good-looking girls," said Miller.

"The girls are all right, only I think they're a little slow on pickin' the right kind. If I had time I'd go over to that church and make a lot o' them Reubs look like thirty-centy pieces. Not that I'm strong on the con talk, but I know I'd be in it with them fellows. I think it must be a case of nerve. That's all there is to 'em — is nerve. But the girls — wow!"

"Beauties, eh?"

"Lollypaloozers!"

II

"It's hard goin' this morning," remarked Artie, as he performed the difficult feat of removing his rubbers without touching his hands to them, "and I ain't much of a mud-horse." He telescoped his cuffs and put them on a hook, yawned lazily and said: "I've got a peach of a head."

"Were you out?" asked Miller.

"Naw, I was settin' in an easy game o' poker. None of us stood to win car fare, but I went in, thinkin' I might get 'em loosened up and pull out the price of a Christmas present for the girl."

"Did you?"

"Well, I should say nit. I think I'll have to duck on that present or else go out with a stockin' full o' sand. You never see such a sure-thing crowd in your life."

"Where were you playing?"

"Over at Kennedy's room. He got me to come over and had a couple of his friends there. Oh, but they was hot members! One of 'em whenever he got better 'n jacks up, always lost his voice and could n't keep count o' the chips. Then he'd stop the game every three minutes to see how he stood with himself. He'd stack up, you know, an' feel in his pockets and then he'd say: 'I'm forty-seven cents loser.' He was the best I ever see."

"Were you playing for money?" asked young Mr. Hall.

"Playin' for —— now, would n't that upper-cut you? Sure. You did n't think this was a game o' muggins, like you boys play up at your little old cycle club? This was the real old army game. I guess I saw as much as two bones change hands."

"How did you come out?" asked Miller.

"Wait and I'll tell you. We kind o' petered along there for two or three hours or so, makin' two call five and as high as fifteen cents to see, everybody keepin' books and beefin' about the way the hands was runnin' and showin' up the cards when nobody come in, and tellin' what they might a' done if they'd done purty well, an' so on — real gambler talk — till I says to myself, 'I'll try it, an' if it do n't go, it's a baby risk.' I gets a pair of typewriters and stays in. All of 'em playin', see? Kennedy leads off. I think he tossed in seven white chips; anyway, he was strong. Then this boy that was keepin' tab on his stack all the time, he had to think it all over and have another talk with himself and skin his cards three or four times, and then he put in. Up to me — see? I kind o' gives the gentle push to half a samoleon and says: 'Comrades, it'll cost you fifty c. apiece to linger in my society.' Say, you never see people so busy. Kennedy has a long talk with himself and counts his stuff, and then he says to this safe player at the right o' me: 'Are you going to call him?' 'Nix,' I says. 'This ain't tennis; this is poker.' Kennedy looked a few spots off his hand, and then he says: 'Well, I'm out,' just as if he said: 'Well, I lose eight thousand on wheat to-day.'"

"Did the other fellow stay?" asked Miller.

"Stay nothin'! He had the heart failure when he see that half. I pulled in the dough and picked up the cards. 'What did you have?' says Kennedy. 'Oh,' I says, 'I did n't have nothin' but five nines.' 'No,' he says, 'on the square, what *did* you have?' I told him it was against the rules for me to say, but it was a cinch I had him done. 'Well,' he says, 'I had three kings.' That ain't no kid, neither. The geezer was settin' there lookin' into three kings all the time."

"Why, he had you beat, did n't he?" exclaimed young Mr. Hall.

"Not in a thousand years. Did n't I tell you I got the stuff — quite a bundle o' money, too. I think there was thirty-six cents. Talk about your Monte Carlo boys! Them guys last night was the gamiest I ever set down with."

"Well, now, did n't you have to tell him what you had?" inquired young Mr. Hall.

"Not accordin' to the league rules for this year. Did I have to tell? You're all right, boy."

"How did you come out?" persisted Miller.

"W'y, what chance did I have to get into 'em? Talk about safe

THE CAUTIOUS BOY

playin'! They're like the stock-yards man that wanted to fight Sullivan. 'I'll fight him,' he says, "if you blindfold Sullivan and gi' me
an ax.' That was the way with them dubs. They liked the color o'
my money, but they would n't take no risk. After that first saucy
crack with the half I laid low three or four hands, and then I
knocked 'em a horrible twister. It was a jack pot, and this cautious
boy at the right o' me opened it. I stay, see? Why should n't I, when
I had two, four, six, seven and nine, in three different colors, all
in my mit? I stands pat on the draw, and then the first crack out o'
the box I whoops it a half — fifty kopecks. What does he do? He
could n't drop his hand too quick. Another case o' licked in a
punch. He shows jacks up for openers and then starts to pick up
my hand, but I stood him off. I says: 'Nay, nay, Pauline, there's
some things so good that it costs money to see 'em.' I told him that
when he wanted to get wise to what was in my hand all he had
to do was to dig up his bit and come in. 'Well,' he says, 'I don't
want to lose my stuff.' On the level, no kiddin,' that's what he said
that he did n't want to lose his stuff. I told him he was in the
wrong kind of a game — that he ought to be playin', 'Heavy, heavy,
hangs over your head.'"

"You have n't told us yet how you came out," said young Mr. Hall.

"Well, I kept on layin' low, and then every fourth hand or so
comin' in with a half-dollar and takin' the pot. Finally, after I'd
sprung it on 'em about a dozen times and was gettin' quite a stack
in front o' me, I stood pat on a hand and tried 'em again. 'Hold on,'
says this cautious boy, shakin' all over, 'hold on, don't take that!' I
told him I would n't take it till it come time. Then him and Kennedy
had a long spiel to themselves. Kennedy was out, of course, not
bein' able to show up better 'n threes. He advised the boy to see
me. Both of 'em looked at the hand and sized me up, and finally
this boy that was holdin' the hand said he'd go halves with Kennedy
and make me spread what I had. They had some more of the talk
and at last they put in a quarter apiece. 'I ain't got a thing but a
flush,' I says, and I lays down four hearts and a diamond."

"That was n't a ——," began young Mr. Hall.

"Sh!" said Miller.

"You ought 'o heard the roar," resumed Artie, giving young Mr.

Hall a reproving glance. "Kennedy hollered the worst of all. 'That ain't no flush,' he says. 'Of course it is,' I come back; 'ain't they all one color?' With that they both begin talkin' at once, showin' me how it was a flush had to be all hearts or all diamonds and that sort o' business. I waited till they got through, and then I said I was dead sore about not bein' next to the point. I says to 'em: 'I been playin' them hands for flushes all night.' The old gag, see? They never tumbled, though. You never heard such kickin'. Them guys thought I'd been playin' red and black hands all the time. This cautious boy figured he could 'a' won four bucks if he'd called me every time I stood pat. Say, you'd died if you'd heard him."

"Well, who won the pot?" asked Miller.

"I think you 're about as bright on the game as they was. W'y, that chump had a full house, nines on somethin'. Soon as he took the half I said I'd stop — would n't play no more till I learned to read the hands. We all cashed in, and what do you think? I was seventy-three cents to the good. There I set like a big stiff for five hours and pulled against them marks for seventy-three cents. Kennedy lose fifty-four cents, an' I'll make a guess right now he ain't through kickin' yet."

III

While they were at lunch a square envelope of a delicate pink color was placed on Artie's table.

It was addressed in very blue ink to "Mr. Arthur Blanchard, Esq."

Furthermore, the stamp was placed upside down on the upper left-hand corner of the envelope. According to the code of the "stamp flirtation" this means either, "Write soon" or "I am longing to see you."

When the recipient is certain as to the feelings of the one who has written, he or she may take this unusual position of the stamp to mean even more than is written in the code.

There may be some ignorant persons who do not know that when a lady passes a handkerchief across her face this is a signal to the gentleman friend, standing in front of the cigar store, that she must speak with him soon.

Again, when a gentleman carries his umbrella grasped by the middle with the handle pointing backward he is making a declaration of love to all women whom he encounters. He may be utterly unconscious of the fact, but any one who understands the leading signals of the "umbrella flirtation" will know what is meant when a gentleman deliberately holds his umbrella in that position.

Furthermore, if he carried his umbrella handle forward and inclined at forty-five degrees it would mean "We must part."

A study of that interesting yellow volume wherein are set down all the secrets of flirtation by means of fan, handkerchief, glove, umbrella, walking-stick, postage stamp, book, etc., etc., will show that a deep significance attaches to the most ordinary procedures. Even the hoisting of an umbrella or the mopping of a damp brow may be construed as an expression of hatred, or the very reverse.

If a young man is too bashful or too diplomatic to make a frank

declaration of love all he has to do is to "crumple the dance programme in his left hand," and the young woman who has studied
the yellow volume will know that he means "I cannot live without
you." (See "programme flirtations.")

Artie no sooner saw the envelope than he smiled broadly. He
knew the meaning of the upside-down stamp, but Miller did not.

"Oh, well, I guess I ain't strong on the North Side," said Artie,
as he held the envelope up to the light. "She writes a swell letter,
don't she? You might think, to size it up, it come from the Lake
Shore Drive. She's a little queer on the spellin', but her heart's in
the right place."

"Is that from one of your lady friends?" asked young Mr. Hall,
with a side wink at Miller. Since Hall had been attending the whist
parties he had shown a disposition to be quietly scornful of Artie's
social connections.

"Never you mind," replied Artie. "This ain't for boys."

He opened the letter and read it carefully, occasionally remark-
ing: "I ain't a bit strong here."

"Are we going to hear it?" asked Miller, who was biting his
pencil with curiosity.

"Not in a thousand. What do you take me for? This letter's for
me and I'm the only boy that gets 'em, too, I'll tell you those."

"That's what she says, I suppose."

"Is that so? I come purt' near knowin' how strong I am with her.
There ain't nobody else one-two-seven. They ain't even in the 'also
rans.'"

"Well, you must be solid."

"Solid? W'y, I'm one o' the family. You could n't queer me with
that girl. I've made the play at the old folks, on the square. The old
man's dead with me. I went to see her one night and she was out,
so I had to set there for about an hour and pipe him the best I
could. Le' me tell you."

Then Artie had to stop and laugh.

'I never put you next to how I come to meet her, did I? Say, there
was the funniest thing ever. It must 'a' been three months ago, a
fellow holds me up for the price of a ticket to a dance up on North
Clark street. I did n't expect to break in, but when the night come

MAMIE

there was nothin' else in sight so I hot-foots up to the dance. It was a sucker play, too, because I might 'a' known it'd be a case of takin' the horse cars to get back to the West Side. I had some new togs, a new pair o' patent leathers and—well, I don't like to star myself, but I guess I was about as good as the best. And this crowd up there was purty-y-y punk; very much on the hand-me-down order."

"It was n't a full dress affair, then?" asked Miller laughing.

"Oh me, oh my! Full dress? W'y, if a guy'd floated in there with one of them Clarence outfits they'd 'a' hung him across a chandelier. Some o' them was dead tough and the others was hams. It was frosty, too. I could n't see any folks I knew, so I stood around there on one foot kind o' rubber-neckin' to find an openin'. Finally I see Mamie over in one corner."

"So that's her name, is it—Mamie?"

"I guess you got past my guard that time. Yes, that's her name, Mamie. As soon as I see her—everything else off. It was a sure enough case of 'only one girl.' 'In a minute,' I says, and I swore I'd get next no matter what kind of a brash play I had to make. Say, she's a dream. That's right. If she had the clothes she'd make the best of 'em look foolish.'"

"I believe you're stuck on her," ventured Miller.

"Mebbe that ain't no lie neither. She'd make anybody daffy. As I was sayin', she was settin' over in the corner, and I could see that a Johnny-on-the spot, with a big badge, marked 'Committee,' was tryin' to keep cases on her. He waltzed with her once or twice, but most o' the time he had to be out on the floor yellin' 'Two more couples wanted,' and all that business. He was makin' himself the whole thing. Well, I got friendly with a guy that was standin' around, the same as myself, tryin' to break in, an' I says to him: 'I want you to do me a favor. Take me over and gi' me a knock-down to the queen in the corner.' He said he didn't know her. 'What's the diff?' I says. 'Ain't you got your nerve with you?' Well, he was all right. He took me over and says: 'Miss Lumyum and-so-and-so,' fakin' it as he went, 'I want you to shake hands with my friend, Mr. Ta-ra-m-m-m,' and then he ducked."

"What was it he called you?"

"He did n't call me nothin'. He just made a bluff. She says to me, 'I did n't ketch the name.' 'Livingstone,' I says, 'Herbert Livingstone. I'm on the board o' trade.' That board o' trade business has been done to death, but I guess it went with her. I asked her for her name and she give it to me—straight. 'How about the next dance?' I says. She said it was all right if Mr. Wilson did n't come around and claim it. I asked her if the boy with the badge owned her and she laughed. I see that he did n't have no cinch on it, so I just started in. I put up the tall talk, jollied her along, danced with her three times—well, of course, you could n't blame her. I sprung them West Side manners o' mine on her and I had her won. Finally his rabs with the banner on his coat comes around and begins to roast her. Sore? You never see a man so sore."

"Why did n't you stop him?"

"Oh, I did n't stop him, did I? Mebbe I let him go right ahead and have his own way. You ought o' seen me. I put up a bluff that'd curl your hair. I went up to him and I breathed it right in his ear. I leaned against him. 'Look here,' I says, 'you screw right away from here. We do n't like your style. If you open your face to this lady again to-night I'll separate you from your breath.' Did he go? Well, I should say yes. He did n't want none o' my game."

"Did n't she get mad?" asked young Mr. Hall, who had become intensely interested.

"What, after he'd weakened that way? His name was pants, then and there. I says to her: 'That fellow's got a horrible rind to think he can set on the same side o' the room with you.' Then she said she did n't know what she'd do, because he'd brought her there and her pa-pah would be crazy if she went runnin' around the street by her lonelies. You see, I was n't doin' all the stringin'. She kept playin' that 'pa-pah' gag on me. Pa-pah wanted her to take music lessons, and pa-pah was very particular who she went out with, and ma-mah was worried whenever she stayed out after twelve. I did n't want to call her down, but I could tell from the dress and the talk and all that that she'd never had any diamonds to throw at the birds. But then I was spinnin' pipe dreams myself, tellin' about how much I lose on the board and all that."

Miller leaned back in his chair and roared. Artie waited for him to subside.

"I took her home, but not all the way. She stopped on the corner and said that was far enough. I sized it up that the house was on the bum and she did n't want me to see it. I had her name and I told her I wanted to write to her. She said, 'Mebbe,' and then she flew."

"Did n't you kiss her good-night?" asked young Mr. Hall, roguishly.

"Well, the——," and what Artie then and there said under an extreme stress of indignation need not be repeated. "Say, do you know who I'm talkin' about? Do n't you make none o' them funny plays at me. I'm tellin' you that this is the first time I met her. I do n't know how they act in your set, but this girl — well, you've got to know her awhile."

"I was just joking," said young Mr. Hall.

"All right, drop it. As I was sayin', I told her I'd write to her, but I did n't. Well, one day on Dearborn street, who does I meet but the girl, comin' out of a buildin' where all them printin' offices are. 'Hello, there, little one,' I says. 'Do you work up here?' That kind o' staggered her. So she weakened and said she did. She ain't a very good liar. I walked down to the corner with her and give her a little song about thinkin' all the more of her since I'd learned she was a workin' girl. She was so square I could n't string her no more, so I told her who I was and fixed it up to take her to a show. Well, when I went out to the house it was a purty small place in behind a grocery store. Pa-pah had on a woolen shirt and was smokin' a pipe. You could see that Mamie was the main screw o' the house and run things to suit herself. The old man's a hard-workin' old boy, and I think I'm strong with him. The old lady's a little leary of me, but I can win her all right."

"Is Mamie the one that you've been calling 'the girl' all the time?" asked Miller.

"She's the only one that got a Christmas present from me. And say," he continued, lowering his voice so that young Mr. Hall could not hear, "if I ever rent a flat she's the party that picks out the furniture. That ain't no josh, neither."

IV

Both Artie and Miller had been kept at the office unusually late because of the extra work that comes at the end of the month. It was nine o'clock when they left. Miller took Artie by the arm and led him toward a billiard hall, where they frequently had fifteen-ball pool contests.

Artie was the better player and usually had to "spot" three.

The corner table was not in use. With the remark that he would proceed to play pool as "old folks" played it, Artie removed his coat, pushed his linen cuffs into one of the sleeves, lighted a fat cigar and began a critical inspection of the cues in the rack. Having selected a cue he carefully deposited his cigar at one edge of the table and "busted" the fifteen balls with a fierce stroke.

When the balls stopped rolling they were scattered all over the table, but not one of them had gone into a pocket.

"A dead rank Jonah," muttered Artie, as he backed away from the table and took a firm bite at his cigar.

When he became deeply interested in a game of pool, and particularly when he was behind in the count, he dropped his usual talkative mood and became silently earnest and watchful.

Miller appeared to have caught a winning stroke, and, although Artie was expected to "spot" three, Miller had four balls before Artie made one. Then Artie became actually serious, pulling his cigar still deeper into his mouth and studying the situation carefully before undertaking a shot.

He did not observe the young man who had drifted over from another table to watch the game until this young man said, in comment on one of Artie's failures: "That's where you ought to have made a bank."

Artie glanced at him sharply. The young man had a dark mus-

THE POOL SHARK

tache, pointed at the ends. His garments bespoke a sporty cheapness and he was smoking a cigarette.

Artie looked at Miller and said: "I wish I knew where I could get some brainy guy to gi' me lessons on this game."

The young man smoking the cigarette pretended not to hear this remark. He leaned against one of the posts and idly watched Miller prepare to make an impossible shot.

Strange to say, Miller made the impossible shot, although the ball did not go into the pocket for which he had vaguely intended it. Miller bore up calmly, as if he were not surprised.

"Oh, sister," moaned Artie, "I got no show for my life with a man that plays like that. Just shut your eyes every time and you've got a cinch."

"That was a lucky play," observed the stranger.

"Oh, I do n't know," said Artie, regarding the stranger with a sidewise glance. "I do n't know."

Miller shot again and went out.

"Now, let's make it a three handed game," said the stranger, coming forward.

Artie stopped short, slowly rubbed his chin and looked at the intruder. "You won't think I'm too fly if I ask you a question, will you?"

"Why, no."

"Well, where did you get your chips to come in here? I ain't seen no one haulin' at you to get you in. Your clothes ain't tore, as I can see."

"Now, there's no need of makin' a roar," said the stranger, with a conciliating smile.

"Ain't there? You're just tryin' to break into the game, that's all. I s'pose you're lookin' for cigarette money."

"Oh, well, if you're goin' to act that way I do n't care whether I play with you or not. I just thought ——"

"Drop it! Do n't try to con me with no such talk. I'm on to you bigger 'n a house. I know about you and the whole push o' ringers. Me and my friend here play a gentleman's game, understand? I might stand some show against you, only I do n't take my meals off of a pool table. I ain't no shark that hangs around these places all day lookin' for somethin' easy, and I'm just foolish enough to think that I'm too good to play pool with a skin like you."

"Oh, you make me tired," said the intruder, who had walked away a few paces and then returned, as he evidently did not wish to retreat while he was under fire.

"Is that so?" demanded Artie, who still had his cigar in his mouth. "W'y, say, I'll make book right here that you're livin' off o' your mother or sister and payin' no board. I know you kind o' geezers like a book. I do n't come in here to give coin to no such stiffs as you. No — no — not if I'm on to my job."

"I guess you've said about enough," remarked the young man with the mustache. His cigarette trembled between his stained fingers.

"Mebbe — but I'm in purty good voice yet, if any one should ask. I just want to put you next to one thing. When any o' you blokies try to push into a game where I am and get me to put up any dough against your shark combinations — w'y, you're on a dead one. I may be a farmer, but it takes better people than you to sling the bull con into me."

The stranger turned half-way around and said: "I do n't care to quarrel with you in here. I'll see you later."

Then he started to walk away.

"Mebbe you will," said Artie, "but you won't be lookin' for me, you big stiff."

And with that he began digging his cuffs out of his coat-sleeve.

"How was it?" he asked, grinning at Miller.

"I thought he was going to fight."

"Not that boy. He was four-flushin', I know the brand."

V

It was not a strange thing, after all — the growing friendship between Miller and Artie.

There is a common theory, and a theory at best, that "birds of a feather flock together," and this may mean that the human being selects for his companions the people who are much like himself in tastes, habits and aspirations.

Nevertheless, a South Side man, who has written a large book intended to be a guide to happiness and sold by subscription only, claims that a tall man should marry a short woman, a blonde should select a brunette, the quiet man should choose for his partner a vivacious woman and the intellectual giant should give the preference to a housekeeper or a cook.

He points out the obvious disadvantages that would result were an artist to be tied up with an art critic, and depicts the misery obtaining in that household every member of which wishes to do all the talking.

Miller and Artie got along famously together. Miller was the listener and Artie was the entertainer. Miller read books and Artie read the town.

Miller secretly believed that Artie was a superficial young man, but he had to admire his candor and his worldly cleverness. Artie liked Miller because he was a font of sympathy and accepted a confidence in a serious way.

Miller knew only one kind of people, and these were the three-button-cutaway, standing-collar, derby-hat people of his own reputable station in life.

Artie had acquaintances in every layer of society.

Artie's casual reflections on matters about town were so many revelations to Miller, whose ignorance, considering that he belonged to a club and had a library of his own, was appalling. Artie's ordinary experiences were thrilling adventures and Artie's love affairs and the briskness with which they were conducted, amazed and interested him.

Miller had always lacked the resolution to have any love affairs of his own.

At the close of an unusually dull day in the office Miller and Artie went to a "new place" to eat. It was a dull week when Artie could not find a new restaurant, and he was especially warm in his praise of this latest discovery, because it offered a complete dinner for the comparatively small sum of fifty cents.

Artie had been in a bad humor all day and had taken out his spite on young Mr. Hall, who had been lolling at his desk throughout the afternoon and writing a long letter to a chum who was attending a school somewhere in the east.

"Who is he — one o' them rah-rah boys with a big bunch o' hair?" asked Artie when young Mr. Hall first spoke of the "chum."

"He's an awfully nice fellow," responded young Mr. Hall, stiffly. He had attended the academy himself and he did not like the reference to "rah-rah boys."

"I'll bet he's one o' them saucy guys that wears a big ribbon. Say, you skipped a couple o' pages there."

Young Mr. Hall, after filling the first page of his letter, had begun writing on the fourth page. He paid no attention to Artie's sarcasm. After he had filled the last page he opened the sheet and began inside, writing crosswise of the paper.

Artie, who had been watching with cold disgust, said: "When your old college chum gets that letter it'll keep him guessin' where to begin on it."

Young Mr. Hall smiled rather contemptuously. "Did n't you ever see a letter written this way?" he asked.

"Certainly not. I've been gettin' letters right along from the nicest people on the South Side and they always begin on the last page and write it backwards. On the level, I'm surprised you ain't on to that. Anybody that'd write that kind of letter could n't play in our set."

"For goodness' sake, stop!" exclaimed young Mr. Hall. "You're getting me so rattled I can't write."

"W'y, sure, only I was tryin' to put you next to some good point-ers. I do n't like to see a nice promisin' boy like you queer himself in sassiety just when he's at the post."

"What do you know about society?" demanded young Mr. Hall.

"Why, Harold, old chap, I know all about it — I know it easy, too. Did n't you see me at the last charity ball?"

"I'd like to see you at a charity ball," said young Mr. Hall, de-risively. He was becoming thoroughly exasperated.

"Oh, I could be there, I guess, if I wanted to. It's a case o' ten bucks and rentin' one o' them waiter suits. I know boys that went down there and put on a dizzy front, and next day they had to make a hot touch for a short coin so as to get the price of a couple o' sinkers and a good old 'draw one.'"

"Well, that's all right: let me finish my letter."

"Go ahead, old fel, I never said a word."

But he kept on nagging the unhappy young man just the same, and Miller wondered at it, for he had never before seen Artie in such an ugly mood.

Therefore, when they had reached the restaurant and Artie con-tinued to be glum and unsociable, Miller asked him the direct question: "What's the matter with you, anyway?"

"O, nothin' much. On the hog, that's all. Been feelin' rotten all day. I did n't want to tell you at the office, but it's all off with me and the girl."

"Who? Mamie?"

"That's the name, all right. She tossed me in the air. She did n't do a thing. I was a great big mark to ever go chasin' after her in the first place. On the square, Miller, I can't get wise to a girl. Too deep, too deep. Just when you think you've got everything nailed down — bing! and it's all off, see?"

Miller admitted that he did n't exactly see. "Have you quar-reled?" he asked.

"Here, I'll give you the whole business. I goes out there last night, gets there about nine o'clock, and who does I meet comin' out o' the house but a cheap gazabo that was with her the first time I see her. I've told you, ain't I, how I snared her away from him?"

"Yes; his name was Wilson."

"Same boy. I told you what he was — a horrible Reub; one o' them fellows that you want to get a crack at the minute you see him. You kind o' feel there's a crack comin' to him. Mame opens the door, and I goes in — purty chilly, too. 'Who's your friend?' I says. She puts on as good a front as she can and says, 'That's Mr. Wilson that was up to the dance that night.' 'Well,' I says, 'he must be a peach to come around here after the way you turned him down.' She tries to pass it off, and says so-and-so and so-and-so about him bein' soft and writin' notes to her all the time. 'Come off,' I says; 'he would n't be writin' notes and comin' 'round here unless he had some pull.'"

"I do n't know about that, Artie," suggested Miller. "Just because a fellow calls on a girl is no sign that she likes him."

"Yes, but this guy's an Indian. He won't do. He do n't belong. It made me crazy to think he'd been cuttin' in there. Mame tried to give me a con talk and that made me sore. 'Look here,' I says, 'I play no understudy to a low card. Now, if you're stuck on him I'll cash in right here and drop out o' the game.' She said she was n't stuck on him, but she could n't tell him to keep away from the house. 'If I ever find him here you won't need to tell him,' I says. 'I'll dig into him and tear him to strips.' Then she says 'Just because I've got other gentlemen friends ain't no call for you to walk on me.'"

"Did she say that?"

"That's what she was gettin' at. I says: 'Nay, nay, Pauline; your own Willie's got to be the whole thing or nothin'. An' I told her if I was beat out I wanted to be done up by somebody besides a counterfeit. Then she cried and said she'd never speak to me again, and I says, 'Well, there are others,' and with that I goes into the hallway, takes my hat off the hook and ducks, and there you are. Everything off."

"No, not necessarily. It seems to me that you quit her, instead of her quitting you. Do n't you think you can fix it up?"

"Say, it *might* be squared," and he spoke rather hopefully, "but there's only one way to fix it with me. That Indian's got to keep clear off o' that street. You can make book on that."

VI

Artie and Miller had gone to a matinée on Saturday afternoon. They very seldom did this, but it was a cold and cloudy day, and on such a day the light and warmth of the play-house seemed very attractive.

After the third act they had walked out to the front of the house and were standing in the lobby, when Bancroft Walters came in very hurriedly and started toward the box office.

Bancroft Walters is the second son of LaGrange Walters, who manufactures a superior kind of roofing and has grown moderately rich at it.

Bancroft plays the banjo, appears at amateur entertainments, goes to a great many parties, and probably belongs to that indefinite class known as "society young men." He has a desk in his father's office, but it cannot be said truly that he is held down to office hours or that his salary represents the value of his actual service. He attended an eastern college for two years, and then came home for some reason, which perhaps only his fond and trusting mother could satisfactorily explain.

She knows it was the fault of the college.

Bancroft is inclined to be dapper, talkative and wonderfully full of self-assurance. Then he has that gift of not discovering that most people regard him as a very ordinary sort of person.

When Bancroft saw Miller and Artie he smiled and said, "Hello, men."

"Why, how do you do, Mr. Walters?" replied Miller.

Artie said nothing.

Bancroft bought his seats and then walked over to Artie and slapped him on the back.

"Well, Artie, have you seen any good mills lately?" he asked.

Artie shrugged his shoulders, tightened his lips and said nothing.

Even then young Mr. Walters did not know that trouble was breeding.

"I haven't seen you for a long time, Artie."

"I seen you since you seen me," replied Artie.

"Is that so?"

"Yes, and I want to tell you somethin', Banny. You're nothin' but a two-spot. You're the smallest thing in the deck. Say, I see barrel-house boys goin' around for hand-outs that was more on the level than you are. Now, I'll put you next to one thing; I want nothin' to do with you, because I'm on. I know you — see?"

"What do you know? What do you mean?" Bancroft was frowning fiercely, but he was also very red.

"Chee-e-ese it! You know what I mean. You can't do nothin' like that to me and then come around afterwards and jolly me. Not in a million! I'll tell you, you're a two-spot, and if you come into the same part o' town with me I'll change your face. There's only one way to get back at you people."

"I guess I know what you're talking about now, but I do n't see that I'm called on to make any explanations," said Walters, who was recovering his voice.

"I do n't want no explanations. I pass you up. All I say is, keep away. I want to mix with white people. I'm very foolish about that, of course, but it 's a way I've got. You 're a nice boy, but your work is very coarse, and I'm givin' it to you right when I say that I 've got a license at this minute to give you a good swift punch."

"Hold on, Artie," exclaimed Miller, seizing his friend by the arm. Miller was pale. He interfered at the right moment, for Artie's anger was up and his fist was in readiness. Walters suddenly turned up his collar and said, in a voice trembling with rage: "I'm not going to have any trouble in this kind of a place."

Then he turned and walked away with the best show of dignity at his command, while Miller still held Artie by the arm and stared at him.

For once he believed Artie to be in the wrong. Bancroft had come up and spoken pleasantly enough, and in return Artie had played the part of a bully seeking a pretext for a fight.

"What made you act that way?" he demanded.

"Do you know that boy?"

"Well, I've met him."

"Yes, but you do n't half know him. I ought o' smashed him before he opened his face."

"What's the trouble between you?"

"Oh, well, let it drop. He knows, though. He knows. And I think he'll remember two or three things I told him. Come on in and let's see the rest of the show."

They did not enjoy the last act of the play.

Artie was still simmering with indignation, and he was also worried to think that Miller had been offended. As for Miller, he could only wonder what Artie had shown such a fierce disposition to fight when there was no apparent provocation.

As they were leaving the theater Artie said: "I think I'll just tell you why I've got it in for that Charley boy. I ain't stuck on tellin' it, for it made me look like a monkey."

"I could n't imagine what was the matter," said Miller. "Walters always seemed to me to be a nice sort of fellow — that is, harmless."

"Harmless? He threw the boots into me the worst I ever got 'em. Ooh! He made me feel like a tramp. Say, Miller, if I was to beat his whole face off I could n't ketch even. He got way under the skin on me. Now, this is on the q.t., but did you ever get the worst of it in such a way that you could n't come back at the time, and yet you was so crazy mad that you could 'a' cried? Well, that was me."

"I'm surprised."

"Was n't I? W'y, I went to school with that guy out on the South Side when my old man had a job in the foundry and old Walters was just beginnin' to get a little dough. The family did n't put on no such lugs in them days. But then, there's no roar comin' on that, because the old man's as common as dirt, and this same two-spot's got a sister that can have my seat in the car any time she comes in. I ain't one o' them beefers that's got it in for people just because they've got the coin and make a front with it. I'm out for the stuff myself. But I do hate to see any of 'em get swelled on account of it."

"Well, now," said Milller, "it never seemed to me that Walters was that kind."

"That's what knocked me the twister. I thought this fellow was all right. I've known him to speak to ever since we learned to smoke cigarettes together back o' the car barns. Here not more'n six months ago he comes into a restaurant where I was settin'. He was with a lot o' them Prairie avenue boys, and purty soon he ducks 'em and comes over an' touches me for two cases. Now, you know you can't go up and bone a stranger for stuff, can you? He knew me well enough to get the two."

"Did he pay it back?"

"Sure he did. I ain't sayin' that he's crooked. I'll tell you when he give it back to me. It was one night out at the boat club when we was havin' some bouts there. I brought over a handy boy from the West Side to put him against a little fellow from the boxin' school. They told me over west the boy was a world-beater, but gee! this North-Sider made a choppin' block out of him. What I was goin' to get at was that Banny was there."

"Who's Banny?"

"That's his name. We used to call him that when he was a kid. Well, he was out there that night bettin' all kinds o' talk, and you'd thought I was his long-lost brother. He stood around the corner where I was handlin' my man, and it was 'Artie' this and 'Artie' that all the time. He loved me that night. Mebbe that's because he had a few under his belt, but anyway it went with me. I thought the boy was all right."

Artie paused in his story and put a large cigar into his mouth. Miller reached into his pocket for a match, but Artie shook his head.

"This is how I found the streak o' yellow in him," said he. "One afternoon the boss sent me out to Grand Crossin' to see a man. I stayed for supper out there and was comin' in on the train along towards eight o'clock. At one o' them stations out there, here comes a whole crowd o' people — a lot o' swell girls and their fly boys. The car was nearly full. I'm alone in a double seat, see? A girl comes runnin' down the aisle and sets down right across from me and says, 'Hurry up and grab this place.' Then who comes up and drops into the seat with her but Banny, understand? I'm readin' the paper, but I drops it and makes the horrible play. I

lifts my derby clear off o' my head and I says: "Good evening!'
Say, he was four feet away. Say, it was just like you there and me
here. This queen with him sees me make the play and kind o'
giggles. Mebbe I did n't do it right. But him — he turned around
sideways in his seat and begins chinnin' her and never sees me at
all. Course, you could n't expect him to. I was nearly three feet
away and lookin' right at him. Miller, this is straight, so help me.
He threw me down. He'd never seen me before. All because he
was out with the swell push and had this queen with him. I
pulled the paper up in front o' me, and I thought my ears'd fry
and fall off. I was groggy. Never did I get it harder. Talk about
a half-hook on the point o' the jaw!"

"It was a confounded shame," said Miller, warmly.

"Say, Miller, am I a vag? Am I fit to ride on a train with other
people? Would a man queer himself by speakin' to me? Now, I
did n't expect no knockdown to his girl. I do n't trot in her class.
But to think of that stiff turnin' on me because I spoke to him.
That's what put the hooks into me. I won't forget it — never. I
was sore, but it was worse'n that. It made me feel rotten."

"I'm not surprised."

"Well, I did n't see him again till today. You heard what I said.
Well, at that, he's got the best of it. I never will be able to give
him the right kind of a hot come-back for what he done to me."

VII

One Saturday afternoon Artie Blanchard was enjoying his half-holiday in a manner peculiar to himself. He was battling with the crowd in State street.

He had his coat-collar turned up and his hat was pulled rakishly forward so that it threatened to produce friction with his eyebrows every time he changed the expression of his face.

He was whistling a little composition that had lately taken possession of his thoughtful moments. It was entitled "I'll Be True to My Honey Boy."

Artie did not know the tune or the words, so he merely whistled it on speculation and when he came to the doubtful parts he hundled.

When he grew tired of whistling he smoked a black cigar.

Artie was apparently at peace with the world and any one to have seen him shift his cigar from the right pocket of his mouth to the left merely by the play of facial muscles would have said, "Here's a young man content."

But Artie, like many other young persons, never whistled more cheerfully, smoked more hungrily and looked into show windows with more seeming interest than when he was keeping company with a great sorrow.

It could have been nothing less than the guiding hand of Fate that shoved him around a bevy of women who were carrying bundles and looking at show windows at the same time, thus contriving to mow down anything and anybody that happened in their way. For Artie immediately got a view of the cause of his sorrow. He would have known her by the sacque alone, but the sprig of plumes on the hat helped in the identification.

Your ordinary lover would have retreated, palpitating. Considering that when Artie had last seen her she was all tears and that his parting words had been, "There are others," it would have

THE CONNELLY GIRLS

been proper for him to drop back into the moving crowd before she turned from the display of precious furs and saw him there looking at her.

But Artie did nothing of the kind.

He walked up to her, brushed some imaginary dust from the bulge of her sleeve, and said: "Hello, girlerino! How's everything stackin'?"

Mamie turned around and there was a leap of color to her face. She said: "Why, Mr. Blanchard."

"What was you pipin' off — the furs?" asked Artie.

"Yes," with her face half-turned from him.

"Do you see the big sealskin sacque there? I was lookin' at it the other day. I'm thinkin' o' buyin' it for a lady friend o' mine."

"Indeed!"

By this time she had recovered somewhat and she spoke with an evident attempt to be coldly sarcastic.

"You heard me, did n't you? I went in and asked the main squeeze o' the works how much the sacque meant to him, and he said I could have it for four hundred samoleons. 'Well,' I says, 'that's a mere bagatelle to me. That would n't keep me in shirt-studs for a month.'"

He paused for a moment or two, watching her all the time, and then he said: "But mebbe you'd rather have that other one up there. You know what you'd like."

Mamie did not look at him and she did not answer. Artie's attempted playfulness was too bearish for her, and Artie seemed suddenly to realize this. He changed his tactics.

"Mame," he said, putting his forefinger softly against her arm.

"Well?"

"Is it fixed up?"

"Is what fixed up?"

"You know."

"No, I do n't."

They were standing side by side, both looking intently into the show-window and talking to it. Their conduct was sufficiently strange to have attracted the attention of the people who brushed against them. But in State street the pedestrians will not give their serious attention to a man unless he does something worthy — such as falling off a cable car or colliding with the tongue of a wagon.

"How about my little old picture. Is it turned to the wall?"

"I — guess not."

"Oh, you're guessin', are you? Well, I s'pose the other boy's fillin' all my dates?"

"That silly thing!"

Artie chirruped as if skeptical. "He's a nice boy," said he, and added, after a deep sigh, "Nit — not."

Mamie turned to him, and, in a quick flame of earnestness, said: "Artie, you know I can't bear that old thing, and I'll never speak to him again as long as I live." She had tears in her eyes.

"You won't be loser anything at that."

"I'm going to write to him and let him know something."

"Why, no; not at all. I've told you all along that if you'd give me his address I'd go around and fix it all up with him."

"If it had n't been for him we would n't have ——"

"Would n't have put on the gloves, eh? Well, come on. Let's be movin'."

He took her by the arm, and then he remembered that it was State street and three o'clock in the afternoon, so he let go.

"I have to meet the Connelly girls in a few minutes. I promised them."

"Shake 'em. You 've got somethin' better than the Connelly girls."

Mamie gave him a vicious nudge in the ribs and broke out laughing, and the war was then and there over, before the tears had dried.

"About Tuesday night, Mame?"

"Yes — or Monday?"

"Good enough. An' now you come right in here and get into line with a bunch o' violets. There's nothin' too rich for the sunshine o' the North Side."

It was not the same Mamie who came out of the florist's wearing violets, and it was not the same Artie who was grinning at her delight over the little present.

"Now, I must go for the Connelly girls," she said.

"All right. Say, Mame."

"Yes."

"I'll just make that to-morrow night."

VIII

At eight o'clock the front room was gently baking with heat from the baseburner, and the gas-jet, with four scalloped dance programmes dangling from it, was lighted to the utmost.

On the marble-topped table was the photograph of a tense young man with plastered hair. The picture lay against a metallic prop of fanciful design which was intrenched between the album and a copy of "Lucille." The swollen furniture was ornately jig-sawed and confined in plush, and every piece of it was modestly backed up against the wall.

The crayon portrait of Mamie's father looked down benignly on this room cleared for action. The portrait represented a bearded top with a fantastic forelock, a neck-tie spotted with great accuracy and a shirt-front bearing a lump of gold. On two or three occasions of his life, Mamie's father had borne an approximate resemblance to the man in the frame.

One occasion was that of the visit to the photographer's and the other was that of the social reception to the executive committee of the Union. In the picture Mamie's father was clean and unwrinkled and he bore a placid, maiden-like expression which Mamie had seldom observed in him.

The crayon portrait had originally been a bargain for $2.50, and the agent who delivered it had put in a frame at $14. The frame was a boiling foliage of white and silver. With such a picture in the house there was no chance for Mamie to lose regard for her father. As for the father, he escaped an affliction of pride by remaining in other rooms of the house.

This crayon portrait dwarfed the "Yard of Roses," the "Wide-Awake" and "Fast Asleep" prints and the other pictures hanging on the walls. It was the luminous thing of the front parlor, and it was to the portrait that Artie Blanchard addressed himself as he came in from the hallway, with his arm lingering at Mamie's waist, half-way between a caress and a hug. "Hello, old boy," said he, and then he asked Mamie, "How does the old gentleman stack up?"

"He's back there now, reading the paper."

"All right. I was n't lookin' for him."

Artie pulled out a chair and seated himself in it sidewise. He happened to see the photograph on the table.

Artie — "Well, I'm not turned to the wall, eh?"

Mamie — "Do n't begin talking that way."

Artie — "I was just kiddin', Mame. How's the ma-mah?"

Mamie — "She was asking about you to-day."

Artie — "Say, on the square, has she got any time for me?"

Mamie (*warmly*) — "Why, of course. She likes you."

Artie — "Well, the ma-mah's got a cold eye in her head. I can't make out whether I'm strong or not. She ain't the kind of a girl that'd be afraid to say a few things if she wanted to."

Mamie — "Pooh!"

Artie — "How about the ringer?"

Mamie — "What's that?"

Artie — "You know — that guy you was goin' to frost. Have you wrote to him?"

Mamie (*excitedly*) — "You mean Mr. Wilson. I hav n't told you, have I?"

Artie — "Well, I should say not. Has he been trailin' you again?"

Mamie — "Not, but he wrote to me. It's the funniest thing you ever read. I'll get you the letter."

Artie — "Gee! That boy's a stayer. If he do n't keep off o' my route there'll be people walkin' slow behind him one o' these days. Let's see what he says."

(*Mamie goes to the adjoining room and returns with a letter and offers it to Artie.*)

Artie — "Go on and spiel."

Mamie (*with a nervous giggle as a preliminary*) — "Well, he begins by saying, 'Miss Mary Carroll, My Dear Madam.'"

Artie — "'My Dear Madam.' Would n't that cook you, though?"

Mamie — "Listen." (*Reads*)

"I do not know why you should have treated me as you have done. I have always regarded you as a friend, but of late I have come to the opinion that you desire to sever our friendship, seeing that you did not speak when I met you last Sunday eve. If you have anything against me I would like to know in what regards I have not treated you right and like a lady. I am very truly, your obedient servant. GRANT WILSON."

Artie — "That's a good thing. I wonder where he got next to that fancy pass about severin' friendships. I'll make that foxy boy think somebody's severed him if I take a crack at him. Did you answer it, Mame?"

Mamie — "Not yet. Would you?"

Artie — "Sure! I'd send him one that'd burn a hole in the mailsack. You get your little old sheet of paper and I'll tip you off a few things to tell that boy. I'll bet you all kinds of money that I can send him somethin' that he'll talk about in his sleep. You get the paper."

(*Mamie goes to the next room and returns with writing material. She removes the photograph album and then seats herself at the table ready to write. An attack of the giggles.*)

Artie — "Chop the laughin'. Go on and write to him. I'll tell you what to say. Just begin this way, 'You 're all right but you won't do.'"

Mamie — "No, no, Artie, please no. I do n't want to say it that way. Besides, I've got to address him first. Now, what shall I call him?"

Artie — "You could call him a good many things and make no error, I'll tell you those."

Mamie — "I know, but shall I say 'Mr. Wilson, Sir,' or just 'Dear Sir?'"

Artie — "Naw, not in a thousand. What do you want to jolly him for? Get in plenty o' rough work right from the start. Throw it into him hard. Call him 'foolish Wilson boy.' You've got to wallop one o' them people to make 'em understand. Just say, 'Get out o' town and keep quiet and you may live to see the flowers again.' If you give him that easy talk he'll think you 're leadin' him on. Let *me* write to his nobs and *I'll* fix him. (*Artie takes the pen and writes for a few moments, Mamie watching him and suppressing giggles.*) Now, how's this? This is the real stuff. (*Reads.*)

" 'I just received your nervy letter. You are all right, but you won't do. Do not come into our ward or I will have you pinched. Remember, I never saw you before in all my life. You are worse than a stranger to me. I would advise you to stop smokin' that double-X brand of dope, because it gives you funny dreams. By fall' off the earth you will oblige.' "

Mamie (*on the verge of hysterics*) — "Oh-h-h-h-h! What *would* he think if I sent him a letter like that?"

Artie — "He'd think he was up against the cold outside, and that's where he is, huh?"

Mamie — "Of course. You know that."

(*Artie drops the pen, and with great caution wraps his arm around her waist.*)

TABLEAU.

IX

On that morning Artie had come in a half-hour late.

His "Good morning, people," was dry and husky, and after he had seated himself at his desk he put his left palm up to his forehead, sighed deeply, and said, without addressing any one in particular: "The boy that wrote that song about 'Oh, what a difference in the morning,' was on to his job. I've got a set o' coppers on me this g.m. that'd heat a four-room flat and my mouth tastes like a Chinese family 'd just moved out of it."

"Another poker party?" asked Miller.

"Guess again. Worse'n any poker party. A bat—real old bat. Pazoo-oo-ooo! Oui! Mebbe you think I ain't got a lulu of a head on me this morning. I ought to be out at the Washin'tonian home with the rest o' them stills and hypos."

"You do n't mean to say that you were—loaded?" inquired Miller, leaning over his desk and lowering his voice so that young Mr. Hall should not hear.

"To the guards. Up to here," and Artie, elevating his chin, drew a forefinger across his Adam's apple.

"Well, I declare," said Miller, and in his voice were both sorrow and reproof.

"Jump on to me," said Artie, as he tried to rub the sleep out of his eyes. "You can't make me feel any sorer 'n I was when I woke up this morning. My head reached out over two pillows. I did n't do a thing to the water pitcher, neither. When I tossed that water into me it sounded like when a blacksmith sticks a red-hot horseshoe into a tub of water. That's no dream, neither."

"How did it happen?"

"How does any o' them things happen? After playin' three or four games o' pool I starts out to get a car and I ain't got it yet. That's always the way—good thing, too. Say, Miller, there ain't many men that go out huntin' a tide. It's a case of meetin' a friend and him sayin' somethin', and then another friend and he loosens, and then you come up, and then the first man thaws again and nobody wants to welch on the proposition, and they keep comin' along and you're a good fellow, see? and do n't want to be a quitter, and the first thing you know you 're up against it, and you do n't care whether there's any night cars runnin' or not."

"Is that what happened last night?"

"About it. I meets Billy Munster, and if you ever trotted a heat with him you know that he's one o'f the biggest jolliers that ever come over the hills, and when it comes to bowlin' — well, he pours a drink that'd make any bar-tender quit bein' sociable. Did you ever try his game?"

"I never heard of him."

"You 've missed a whole lot. He's got a job over at the city hall. I never see him do a stroke of work, but he can always make a flash o' the long green, and I guess it's easy money, too, from the way he lets go of it. I've heard he gets his bit on nearly every good thing that comes along. What his pull is I never could figure out. Every time I see him over at the city hall he's whisperin' to one o' them red-necked boys and fixin' it up to give somebody the double-cross. At that, he's a good fellow. I think he'd mace a sucker if he got half a chance, but after he got the dough he'd spend it freely. That's the kind of a boy he is, and last night he had a roll that you could 'a' stopped up a window with. The minute I meets him he steers me into a joint, makes me heave in a couple and then says: 'Come on; I 've got a good thing for you.' 'Nit,' I says, because I knew his gait. I says: 'I've seen enough o' them sunrises over old Lake Michigan.' 'No,' he says; 'on the level; we'll just drop into the music hall and stay a little while.' So I goes."

"You ought to have gone on home."

"Sure; we all know that the next day. But I goes just the same. We had n't been in there ten minutes till Billy dug up a 'longshore-man with gold in her teeth and was buyin' beer for her. He kept 'em comin' fast and I could n't dodge 'em. Purty soon I was joinin' in the chorus, and I guess from that stage o' the game they did n't have to pull at me to keep me up and comin.' When the song-bird

THE BATTLE-AX

come out to do her turn I could see two of her. I guess this girl that
Billy knew spotted us for a couple of easy marks, for she floated
away somewhere and come back with a friend o' hers."

Artie stopped in his narrative and gave a low, buzzing whistle.
"You ought to seen her."

"Why?" asked Miller, and he had to smile in anticipation.

"Say, there was a battle-ax if ever you see one. She had a face on
her that'd fade flowers. It had one o' them calcimine hard finishes.
You can guess how far along I was when I did n't shy at it. And oh,
the haughty front that she put up. She said she was an actorine.
'What troupe?' I says. 'Well,' she says, 'at present I'm restin'.' I'll
bet a dollar she never done nothin' on the stage but carry a shield,
but to hear the guff she was throwin' out you'd think she could
make Ellen Terry look like a Friday night amatoor. Oh, she was
a bird. I think her name was Gladys. If she come in this room now
I'd jump out o' that window, and last night when I was sloppy I
thought she was the best ever. That just goes to show what the hop-
juice'll do for you."

"How long did you stay there?"

"Till the whole works was closed. I bought drinks for this pelican
friend o' mine till she hollered for me to stop, and then I says to
Billy, I says: 'Let's take the ladies out and give 'em a little supper.'
That was me said that, understand? It was only a little after midnight, you know — the mere shank o' the evening — and I could n't
think o' startin' home as early as that. Oh, no. Little Artie had to go
and give the ladies some supper. You know how liberal a guy is
about that time o' night. He do n't like to take no money home with
him. Billy was right with me, of course. He's a stayer from Stayers-
ville. We got out o' the music hall — I remember that — and the
next thing I can cipher out was that we got to the restaurant and I
was pleadin' with my tall friend to just go right ahead and order
anything she wanted. Well, she was fly enough to do that. Little
Gladys was more'n seven. I think it'd be about an even-money
break that she's seven times seven. She ordered nearly everything
on the bill and I guess I went to sleep with my face in a plate.
That's after Billy had ordered two or three more rounds. Oh, he's
a wonder, that boy. I do n't know where he stows it.'

Artie took a full breath and once more felt of his head.

"Thats about all I remember," said he, "except payin' the check and havin' Billy take me over to the hotel. It must 'a' been three o'clock when I got to bed and I pounded my ear till past seven. I've had a nice breakfast. It was a tall tub o' seltzer lemonade. Talk about old R. E. Morse; I'm full of it this morning. This is the first time I've had a day-after head in many moons, and if you ever ketch me with another one you can take a ball club and hammer the life out o' me. Now, that goes."

"What do you think Mamie would say if she knew you had been out with this other girl?" asked Miller, rather severely.

"Stop it, Miller. Do n't go to rubbin' it in. I got trouble enough to-day without thinkin' o' that. If she'd ever saw me with that fairy I would n't be deuce high with her now. You could n't blame her neither. What do you think of a chump that'd pass up a four-time winner to go and play his money against a sellin' plater, and a has-been at that? I did n't put you on to the good thing though, did I? Last night I had nine cases. This morning when I frisked myself I could n't turn up only sixty cents. I just fed eight big iron louies into that game last night. I do n't know how I'll ever keep up the bluff o' workin' to-day. How do I look?"

"You look knocked out."

"Well, I feel the part."

X

"I've got it to do," said Artie, "and I s'pose I'd better put on the best front I can and play it out."

"There's nothing to be afraid of," suggested Miller.

"Do n't tell me nothin' about that game. I know just what it'll be. On the dead, I'd give a ten-case note to be out of it, but Mame would n't have it that way. She said she'd promised the Connelly girl, and there you are. I'm goin' to be the head knocker in the push. It's a case of gettin' a day off and seein' the thing through from soda to hock. We got to meet at the house and go from there in a carriage."

"You'll enjoy it," said Miller, smiling.

"What, doin' the slow march up the aisle and then standin' there while the main guy spiels and all that business? Not on your tintype. I'll make a miscue somewhere; you see if I do n't."

"You'd better get used to it and find out how it's done. Some of these days you'll have to go through the mill yourself."

"Say, that's what I told Mame, and you ought o' seen her. She blushed up and got rattled and could n't say a word."

"She understood what you meant, did n't she?"

"Well, I guess she was keen enough to make a good, warm guess at it."

Miller gazed at Artie for a few moments and then said: "It's none of my business, Artie, but — you two are engaged, are n't you?"

Artie swallowed something and seemed to be considerably embarrassed.

"Miller," said he, confidentially, "you've asked me a hard one. On the level, I do n't know whether we've got it fixed up or not. You know my style of play. I can kid all right, but when it comes to makin' a dead serious play I'm a horrible frost. I'm the worst

that ever come up the pike. Between you and me and the desk
here, I think she knows that it's goin' to be a marry as soon as
things come right. But as for me ever comin' to the scratch and
sayin', 'Here, how is it? Do you want to open my mail? w'y, I never
had the face to do it yet."

"I thought you had nerve enough to do anything."

"Miller, let me put you next to somethin'. I know a bad man on
the West Side that can lick his weight in wildcats and bluff any
four or five common dubs, and he's got a wife that weighs about
ninety pounds that'll give him just one look and he'll crawl under
a table. He's dead stuck on her, and she can do anything she wants
to with him. It ain't that he ain 't got nerve enough. What is it,
then? Huh?"

"You're getting too deep for me, Artie," said Miller, shaking his
head. "What I meant was that I thought you knew Mamie so well
you could be perfectly free and candid with her."

"I'm an easy runner till it comes to the high jump and then I quit
cold. I can jolly and have fun and put my arm around her, but
when it comes to takin' her by the mit and doin' the straight talk
— nit, and again nit. Two or three times here lately I've said to myself: 'W'y, you big stiff, brace up and get through with it before
you go daffy.' Then I think I'm all right, see? But as soon as I get
with her all that brace fades on me and I say: 'What's the good?
Next week'll do just as well.' Besides, would n't I make a picture if
she'd stand me off?"

"It seems to me that when she asked you to stand up with her
at this wedding that was about as strong a hint as you could ask.
You do n't expect her to come right out, do you?"

"No, but I feel a good deal like a guy that I meet out at the boat
club. He says that if he asked a girl to marry him and she said
'yes,' he'd begin to think her judgment was purty rotten. I do n't
s'pose anybody on top of earth can beat my time with Mame, but
what she sees in me to get stuck on is what keeps your Willie boy
guessin'."

"What does any woman see in any man?" asked Miller, gravely,
somewhat gratified that Artie had taken up with a social theme of
such magnitude.

"Sometimes she sees a roll o' the long green," replied Artie, "but Mame must have good eyesight if she can find any pile belongin' to me. You can turn them X rays on to my bank-book and not find enough dough to fit up a flat."

"She's not after your money."

"No, you can gamble she ain't. I s'pose it's because I'm young and good."

"Yes, because you never drink or stay out nights."

"Break away! I'm tryin' to forget all about that. That's one rea- son I give in to Mame on this weddin' proposition. I felt so ornery about the night that me and Munster laid open the town that I'd 'a' done most anything to get even with myself. She said the Con- nelly girl and her had gone to school together and had been travelin' as a team, and that Florence would n't have nobody else to play first mate when the thing was pulled off. And she says: 'You do n't want nobody else to stand up with me, do you?' That kind o' jolted, and I told her I was n't stuck on puttin' in an under- study, and so I promised to go against the game."

"Do you know this girl that's to be married?"

"I've seen her two or three times, but she always had the mash along. The two of 'em went with Mame and me over to Turner Hall one night. Oh, but they was gone on each other. His name's Tommy Bradshaw and he runs a cigar store. They say he does a nice little business and belongs with the real boys, but every time I ever see him he was a lobster. You could n't drag him more'n six feet away from his sure thing. He kept tab on her every minute. He'd set there holdin' her fan and whisperin' to her, and he did n't want no one else to cut in. I thought his work was very coarse. There's no need of a man goin' nanny just because he's copped out a nice girl all for himself."

"Well, Artie, when a man's in love you can't hold him account- able."

"That's no dream, neither. Any one that's got his head full o' the girl proposition 's liable to go off his trolley at the first curve. I would n't believed it six months ago, but if that North Side won- der'd turn on me now and gi' me the marble heart, I tell you it's a safe money guess that I'd go and jump in the lake."

"Yes, and your old friend Wilson would be back courting Mamie."

"Yes, he would, would he? If she ever passes me up it'll be for some guy that hauls a good deal more freight than that Indian does."

XI

A large yellow rose drooped from Artie's lapel as he came into the office on Thursday morning.

"Hark, I think I hear them weddin' bells.
Tingaly-ting, tingaly-ting, ting-ting-ting."

As he sung this, he put one hand behind his ear and stood in the listening attitude so commonly affected by neat song-and-dance artists.

"Aha! The best man, I believe?" said Miller, moving back from his desk and regarding Artie's specialty with keen delight.

"You know it," replied Artie, "you know it. I was the stroke oar at the doin's, and while I ain't throwin' any bouquets at myself I must say that me and Mame was the hit o' the piece."

"You got through all right, then?"

"A little slow on the get-away, but I made a Garrison finish. I was runnin' in strange company, too, but as soon as I got the pace they could n't head me."

"Tell me all about it. You and Mamie really stood up with them, did you?"

"Did we? Ain't I tellin' you that we done the pacemakin'? I give Mame a wad o' roses that laid over anything the bride could flash, and mebbe you think she was n't in good form. Oh, doctor! She looked out o' sight! Some of 'em have got their sealskins and their sparklers, but this little girl, with that new make-up and the flowers, beat the best of 'em. I'll back her against all comers, bar none. Talk about your peaches, why, she's a whole orchard! That's no Hungarian joke, neither."

"By George, Artie, you are hard hit," said Miller, laughing.

"You're dead right there, an' I make no bones about it. She's got me landed and strung. Say, you must think I'm a prize gilly to set around here and give up my insides to you about her, but I'll tell you, Miller, you're the only man that I'd tell some things to, and I cough up to you because I know that you're a good fellow — and understand that — puttin' aside all this kid talk ——"

"That's all right, Artie. You need n't be afraid of me telling any one. There is nothing to be ashamed of, anyway. Every man falls in love sooner or later."

"Love! There's a word that makes me weary, but on the square, that's what I've got. It's a sure-enough case. Where's Hall?"

"I think he 's out collecting to-day."

"I'm glad of it. I do n't like to say too much in front o' that boy. He do n't know any more'n the law allows, and since he's started to that dancin' school I think he hears funny noises under his bonnet."

"Are you going to tell me about that wedding?" asked Miller, impatiently.

"Well, it was a bird. We did n't break into the sassiety notes, but that cuts no ice in our set. It took all day to pull it off. Mame told me to come straight to the Connelly house, because she had to go there early in the morning. Her and the other Connelly girl was handlin' the bride. It was nearly ten o'clock when I got there, and there was a big push in the front room — Mame's mother, old man Connelly, Mrs. Connelly, Tommy Bradshaw — he was the main guy, you know — one o' Tommy's brothers from the South Side and a chilly mug by the name of Parker, some relation to Tommy. This frosty party was doin' the touch-me-not business all day, an' you could n't get him to take his gloves off. Tommy — new suit, new white necktie, new dicer, new shoes. When he'd lean back and throw one leg over the other, just to show that he was takin' it dead easy, you could see the yellow soles o' them shoes. He was washed and combed till he did n't look right. Say, you could smell the bay-rum clear across the room. I think he overdone it, myself. And say, you ought o' seen him when Mame's mother started to throw the harpoon into him."

"The harpoon?" inquired Miller. He had known Artie for a long time, but occasionally the boy was too versatile for him.

"Sure, the stringin' business. That old girl's a wonder. You see, here was Mrs. Connelly settin' there snifflin' and drippin' around

as if she was goin' to bury the daughter instead of stakin' her to a
cigar store. That worried old man Connelly, and so Mame's mother
tried to jolly the crowd up by playin' horse with Tommy. She'd say:
'Well, Mr. Bradshaw, you're a very handsome man in your new
clothes,' and then throw me the wink. Then she'd ask him if he'd
back out if he had the chance and how many girls he'd been engaged to before. She had him balled up till he could n't say a
word. No use, though; Mrs. Connelly kept moppin' her eyes and
every little while sayin' 'Ah-h-h-h,' like that. I guess it was n't put
on, though. She was probably broke up. Women are different."

"Oh, yes," assented Miller, "she hated to lose her daughter."

"I do n't believe it was that. She claimed it was the happiest day
of her life, and then as soon as she said it she commenced to leak
again. But you ought o' seen old man Connelly. Oh, he's a great old
tad — has charge o' the wagons for one o' them Franklin street
wholesale houses. They say he makes good money. Well, yesterday
he was up against a new proposition. He was all togged out and
had a collar that was chokin' the life out of him. All he could do
was to wipe his mouth on the back of his mit and kind o' trail after
the others. What do you think? At the church he wanted to slide
into a back seat and let the rest of us go up front. 'Come on,' I says;
'be a good fellow and stay with us.' He said he could see all right
from where he was, but his wife yanked him out and made him
stick."

"When did you get to the church?"

"It was after twelve o'clock, all right. W'y, we give a parade —
three carriages we had. I had n't hardly had a chance to see Mame
in her new clothes till we got in the carriage with Florence and
Tommy. Florence had about twenty yards o' this mosquito-bar
stuff hangin' to her and was made up great, but even at that she
could n't get better'n place with Mame in the runnin'. She's a nice
girl, though. I do n't want to back-cap her. She was rattled and so
was Tommy. All the way to the church they did n't say more'n
twenty words, and that was about how glad she was the sun had
come out and wantin' to know if Mr. Parker was in the carriage
behind. Tommy grinned and looked foolish. To tell the truth I got
kind o' nanny myself when we stopped in front of the church and

piled out. Mame was all right, though. She froze to me and steered me through without an error. There was a wait just inside when old man Connelly balked on 'em, but after that everything went smooth. About a dozen ringers followed us in and stood around rubberin'."

"Well, what did you have to do?" inquired Miller, with growing interest.

"I done nothin' but stick to Mame. All but us four got planted in front seats and looked on. There was a long spiel by the high guy in the pulpit, and we shifted two or three times, and that's about all I know, except that Tommy agreed to a lot o' business that's enough to set any boy a-thinkin' if he goes against the game. Oh, I forgot. It was right in the dead serious part, just when Florence and Tommy put their lunch-hooks together. 'They're off,' I whispered to Mame, and she came purt' near bustin' out and queerin' the whole act. She roasted me good and hard for it afterwards."

"What did you do after the ceremony?"

"Say, the ceremony was just the first part o' the show. When we got out o' the church Florence's mother was cryin' again and kissin' everybody except me and the old man. We ducked on her. They loaded up the carriages again and all but us four went back to the house. We went over to get some photographs."

"Oh, I see."

"Well, I should say so. You've always got to have one o' them bride-and-groom pictures in the house whether there's anything to chew or not. They wanted me and Mame to go along, so we rode over and watched 'em. Tommy was all right by that time. He'd got his nerve back, and he was real Charley-horse, joshin' me and Mame, and sayin' 'That's all right. Some time I'll come and see you two hitched up.' Was n't that a raw deal, huh? There I was— I'd never said nothin' to Mame about the marry deal, and he was takin' it for granted that everything was set. He was too new about it. I never did like his work. But Mame—say, she passed it off smoother'n silk. She just give him the ha-ha and says: "That'll be all right. You'll get your bid when the shootin' match comes off'"

"She did n't call it a 'shootingmatch'?"

"Naw! I'm just tellin' you, you know. Well, they got their pic-

tures, her a settin' down with the flowers in her lap and him standin'
behind with one of his fins kind o' hid in that mosquito bar. Then
we all drove back to the house to feed our faces."

"Oh, you had a wedding dinner?"

"Did we? That was where I cut loose. That was where I got
good. I made a speech, just for a kid, you know, but it started 'em
— all but that cold guy. I did n't get away till nine o'clock. We fed
an' then we smoked and danced, and old man Connelly played the
flute — rotten, thank you. Mame was the star, too. Do n't forget it.
Honest, we had a good time. Them people up there's good enough
for me. No frills, but they 're on the level, and when it comes down
to cases they're just as good as a lot of people that make a bigger
front. They got hearts in the right place. It's like a man out at the
boat club says, 'If you can't travel with the bell-cows, why stick to
the gang.' That's wise talk, too."

XII

After a hurried luncheon at one of the places where patrons help themselves and compute their own checks, Miller and Artie took a walk on the sunny side of the street.

Artie was not as talkative as usual, and, as Miller seldom did more than encourage a conversation once started, the two sauntered for several minutes in silence.

Then Artie spoke abruptly. "Miller," said he, "I got a hen on."

"What is it?"

"It's like this. Would you dally with politics if you thought you stood to win out a good thing?"

"That depends. *You're* not going into politics, are you?"

"They've got me entered, but I don't know whether I'll start or not. I'm leary of it; I do n't mind tellin' you those."

"What do you mean?"

"Well, mebbe you won't understand. I do n't like to feature myself, but in that precinct where I hang out I'm purty strong. I'm a good mixer and I've kind o' got next to the live ones, and if I do say it myself I think there's a lot of the boys that'd vote my way if I went after 'em hard. Do you know Jim Landon?"

"Who is he?"

"He's the main squeeze in our ward, or any way he used to be. He's one o' the aldermen, and he's out for it again, but good and scared that he can't win out. He come to me last night at Hoover's cigar store and give me a big talk. What he wants is for me to come to the front for him strong. He knows I've got a drag in the precinct, and he says if I'll jump in and do what I can for him he'll see that I got a good job in the town offices, where I can cop out about twice what I'm gettin' now. Of course I'm out for the long green — but I do n't know about this deal."

"Does he stand a good chance of being elected?"

THE MAIN SQUEEZE

"That's what keeps me guessin'. Two years ago he win in a walk, but this spring he had to do all kinds o' funny work to get the nomination. There's a lot o' people in the ward that's got their hammers out and they're knockin' him all they can. They'll put a crimp in him if things come their way."

"What's the matter with him, anyway?"

"Oh, they kind o' think he's done too well. Two years ago he was on this uppers and now he's got money to burn. There's some o' them guys out in our ward can't make out how it is that Jimmy can afford to buy wine at four bucks a throw when he's only gettin' three a week out o' the job. They say they can't stand for that kind o' work, and so there's a lot o' them church people that boosted him two years ago that's out now to skin him. They 've put up a new guy against him and he's makin' a nasty fight."

"I don't understand yet what they've got against your man."

"W'y, they're crazy at him. You see two years ago he made the play that if they put him in he was goin' down to the city hall and change the whole works. He was goin' to clean the streets and jack up the coppers and build some schoolhouses. Jimmy says to 'em; 'Throw things my way and I'll be the Johnny-on-the-spot to see that everything's on the level.' The talk was so good it went. Well, you know what happened to Jimmy when he got down there with them Indians and begin to see easy money. He had n't been in on the whack-up six weeks till he was wearing one o' them bicycle lamps in his neck-tie and puttin' in all his time at the city hall waitin' for the easy marks to come along and throw up their hands."

"I see. He turned out to be a boodler, eh?"

"I do n't see no way o' gettin' past it. I like Jimmy. He's one o' them boys that never has cold feet and there's nothin' too good for a friend, but, by gee, I guess when it comes to doin' the nice, genteel dip he belongs with the smoothest of 'em. And he learned it so quick, too. Ooh!"

"Artie, that kind of a man is a thief and that's all you can make out of it," said Miller, with presbyterian severity.

"Mebbe that ain't no lie, neither. He would n't go out with a piece o' lead pipe or do any o' that strong-arm work, but if Jimmy saw a guy puttin' dough into his pocket he would n't let on. You would n't have to feed him no knockout drops to make him take the coin, I guess. But the nerve o' the boy! He won't never let on that he's handled any crooked money. When he was staked to the office he did n't have a sou markee except what was tied up in a bum little grocery store. Now he's got too strong to tend store and his brother-in-law's running' it. He do n't do a thing in the world except travel around with some more o' them handy boys and lay for jack-pots. And the talk he gives you! Mamma! He's better 'n any o' them shell-workers that used to graft out at the gover'ment pier. W'y, he can set down and show you dead easy that he done all that funny votin' because it was a good thing for the workin' boys. Sure! That's why he wants to stay in, too — so as the tax-payers won't get the short end of it. On the square, if I had his face I'd start out sellin' them gold bricks to Jaspers."

"You do n't mean to say that he has any chance of being elected again?"

"Oh, he's got a chance all right. He's gone right down into his kick and dug up the long green and he's puttin' it out at the booze joints. Some o' the saloons he's overlooked for a year or two, and he's got to make good with 'em to keep 'em from knockin'. But he'll have the whole push rootin' for him, and, then, of course, there's a lot more o' people say: 'Oh, well, Jim's a good fellow and he's been white with me, and even if he does sandbag a few o' them rich blokies what's the diff?' I think he's got a chance, all right. I would n't like to start in and plug his game and then find myself on a dead one."

"Artie, if you take my advice you'll keep out of it. What do you want with a political job?"

"Well, for one thing I want to get a bank-roll as soon as I can and this place he's holdin' out pays good money."

"Yes, and even if you got it you'd be out again in a year or two and worse off than ever. Besides, I would n't help elect a man who sold his influence." Miller spoke with considerable feeling.

"As for that," resumed Artie, "you need n't think I like Jim Landon's way o' gettin' stuff. It's just like this, though. He's gone out of his way two or three times to do things for me and fixed me for a pass to Milwaukee once, and, of course, them things count. Everybody's shakin' him down this spring, and if he gets the gaff he'll be flat on his back. If I did n't know him I'd be against him hard. But you do n't like to throw down a man that's treated you right, do you?"

"I've never been in politics, but I should say that no young man could have any excuse for voting for a boodler."

"Say, now listen. It comes election day, see! I go in the place and get in one o' them little private rooms and I vote for this stranger. Then I come out and meet Jimmy. He puts out the hand and I go and get a cigar with him and do the friendship act. Would n't that be purty coarse work?"

"It would n't be any worse than his promising to be honest and then turning out a boodler" said Miller.

"Well, I guess I'll pass up the whole thing. Come to size it up, that ward's goin' to be floatin' in beer the next two weeks, and I'm not stuck on standin' around with them boys that smoke them hay-fever torches. For a man that do n't want to be a rounder, it's too much like sportin' life. I did n't think you'd O.K. the scheme. That's an awful wise move, too. I guess an easier way to get that roll'd be to borrow a nice kit o' tools and go 'round blowin' safes."

XIII

'Where's he at?" asked the over-grown messenger boy, who had clumped slowly along the hallway and who now entered the room, leaving the door open behind him.

"Ain't he good?" asked Artie, turning to Miller, who was gazing at the messenger with a look of pained surprise in his eyes.

"Where's he at?" repeated the messenger boy.

He seemed rather large and old to be in the uniform, for there was a scrabble of soft beard on his chin. His face and hands appeared to have been treated with fine coal-dust, his cap leaned forward on one side of his head and whenever he spoke he had to make new disposition of a large amount of chewing tobacco which he carried in his mouth.

When he asked "Where's he at?" he pronounced it "where 'ce," and in all his subsequent talk he gave the "s" a soft and hissing sound well prolonged, to the evident enjoyment of Artie and the mild wonderment of Miller.

"Where's who at?" demanded Artie, adopting a frown and a harsh manner.

"W'y, t'e four-eyed nobs dat sent me out on t'e Sout' Side."

"Are you the same little boy? Would n't that frost you, though, Miller? This is little Bright-eyes that took the note for Hall."

"Aw, what's eatin' you?" asked the boy, giving a warlike curl to the corner of his mouth.

"Oh, ow! listen to that. I'll bet you're the toughest boy that ever happened. What you been doin' all day — playin' marbles for keeps or standin' in front o' one o' them dime museeums?"

"Aw, say; you t'ink you're fly. Dat young feller sent me all t'e way to forty-t'ree ninety-t'ree Callamet av'noo. I could n't get back no sooner."

"Who was it the note was to?"

"His rag, I guess."

"Oh-h-h-h! His rag! What do you think o' that, Miller? Ain't this boy a bird! Can you beat him? Can you *tie* him? Boy, you're all right."

"So are you — dat is, from y'r head up."

"An' the feet down, huh? You're one o' them 'Hully chee, Chonny,' boys, ain't you? You're so tough they could n't dent you with an axe."

"Is dat so-o-o-o?" asked the boy, with a frightful escape of "s" and a glare such as he must have used to terrify all the smaller boys at the call station.

"If I was as tough as you are I'd be afraid o' myself, on the level."

"You t'ink you're havin' sport wit' me, do n't you? I seen a lot o' dem funny mugs before dis."

"W'y, Claudie, I would n't try to josh you. I think you're a nice, clean boy. Ain't you goin' to take off your gloves?"

Miller leaned back in his chair and howled with laughter.

"I beg y'r pardon, Claudie," continued Artie. "I thought them was gloves you had on. Gee, is them your mits? You're a brunette, ain't you?"

The messenger boy had been somewhat taken back by the allusion to his "gloves," but he recovered and said, still gazing at Artie: "S-s-ay, you're havin' all kinds o' fun wit' me, ain't you? Well, w'at you — anyt'ing you say cuts no ice wit' me."

"You'd better smoke up or you'll go out," suggested Artie. "You was a little slow on the come-back that last time. Get on to him, Miller; he's lookin' a hole in me."

"He has a bad eye," said Miller.

"Yes, and as the guy says on the stage, I do n't like his other one very well, neither. I'll bet he'd be a nasty boy in a fight. I'd hate to run against him late at night. Them messenger boys is bad people. Guess what they train on."

"I do n't know," said Miller.

"Cocoanut pie. That ain't no fairy tale, neither. Cocoanut pie and milk, that's what they live on. I'll bet Claudie here with the face has got about three cocoanut pies wadded into him now. How about it, Claudie?"

"Say," began the messenger boy, nodding his head slowly to emphasize his remarks, "I'd give a t'ousand dollars if I had your gall."

"That'll be all right. Keep the change. By the way, old chap, are you lookin' for any one?"

This was another surprise for the boy.

"Yes-s-s, I'm lookin' for some one," he replied.

"Who is it?"

'W'y, t'e fellow dat wears de windows in his face. I got a note here for him," and he pulled it out of his pocket.

"Looks like you've been chewin' it. That's his desk over there. He got dead tired o' waitin' for you and went out to tell the police you was lost. I think they're draggin' the lake for you now."

"Aw, go ahead; dat's right. Dere's lots o' you blokies t'ink you can have fun wit' us kids."

"Get next to the walk, Miller; get on, get on!" exclaimed Artie, as the messenger boy moved over toward Hall's desk. On the way he stopped for a moment and spat copiously into a waste-basket.

"He walks like he had gravel in his shoes, do n't he?" said Artie. "Look at the way he holds them shoulders. Ain't he tough, though?"

"Some day you'll get too gay an' a guy'll give you a funny poke," remarked the messenger boy, as he slowly settled into young Mr. Hall's chair and again directed what was supposed to be a terrorizing stare at Artie.

"What did I tell you, Miller? Claudie's a scrapper. He'd just as soon give a guy a 'tump in de teet' as look at him."

The boy gave a sniff of contempt and began an examination of the papers on Mr. Hall's desk, picking up some of the letters and studying them, his lips going through the motions of reading. Artie sat, with face illumined, and watched the boy. He was evidently fascinated by the display of supreme impudence.

"Ain't there nothin' we can do for you?" he asked. "Miller's got some private letters you can read when you get through over there."

"Aw, go chase yourself," replied the boy.

"Well, Claudie, I've seen a good many o' you boys, but you're

YOUNG MR. HALL

the best ever," remarked Artie. "If Hall's tryin' to win out any South Side lady friend I do n't see as he could do better than send you out with the note. I think you'll be liked wherever you go. Gee! you've got that icehouse stare o' yours down pat. If you keep on springin' that you'll scare somebody one o' these days."

"Aw, let go," said the boy in evident disgust. "When do I get to see t'e fellow dat sets here? Won't one o' youse pay me?"

"Miller, pay the boy and let him go. He ain't had any cocoanut pie for nearly an hour now, have you, Willie — er — Claudie, I mean. What is your name, Claudie?"

"What's it to you?"

"Nothin' much, only I wanted to know. You've kind o' won me out. Here! Do n't move! I'll bring the waste-basket over to you."

At that moment young Mr. Hall came in and said: "Ah, boy, have you that note for me?"

"S-s-s-ure. Where you been at? You're helva duck to keep a kid waitin' here. You've got o' pay me ten cents more."

"Do n't be saucy," said young Mr. Hall, severely.

"Aw, rats!"

"You ain't mad, are you, Claudie?" asked Artie, as the boy laboriously moved toward the door, making noises with his feet.

"Oh-h-h, but you t'ink you're a kidder," replied the boy, with a sour smile.

"Look out! You'll step on one o' your feet there in a minute."

Then they heard him go clump-clump-clump out through the hall and away.

"Confound such a boy!" exclaimed young Mr. Hall.

"Oh, he's all right," said Artie, "only you ain't used to his ways."

"He's tough enough," suggested Miller.

'Yes," said Artie, "I would n't be as tough as he thinks he is — not for a million dollars."

XIV

"Let's walk out a little while and let the wind blow on us," said Artie, when the conversation had begun to lag.

He had found Mamie on the front stoop with her father and mother. It was the first warm night of the early spring, and the tired people all along the street had come into the open air, the older ones to sit around the doorways and the children to romp on the sidewalks.

Gas lamps are far apart in that street and the houses are much alike — two stories high, many of them having the high stoop that leads steeply from the sidewalk to the upper story. A stranger might have had some trouble in finding the Carroll house, but Artie knew the neighborhood. He collided with the children and said: "Do n't run me down, kids." There was a carnation in his buttonhole and he clicked a walking-stick on the uneven sidewalk. The smell of pipe smoke, the balm of the cooler evening air and the awakened cheerfulness of the street, which he had never before seen so lively, harmonized with his own feelings. There was a spring song going in his heart, and when he came to the Carroll stoop it strove to find utterance in words.

"Ain't this a James-dandy of a night?" he asked, removing his hat. "I see all you good people are takin' it in."

Mamie arose to greet him, and said something in a low tone to her father. Artie knew what it was.

"Stay where you are, Mr. Carroll," said he. "I'll grab off a place here at the end."

"Father was so warm he just took off his coat and came out here to enjoy his pipe," said Mamie, in way of explanation.

"I do n't blame him. Would n't you rather have a cigar, Mr. Caroll?"

"Well, I do n't mind. Have y' another?"

"Sure thing. You need n't be afraid o' that one. It's got real tobacco in it. How are *you* to-night, Mrs. Carroll?"

"I'm all right now, but this afternoon I thought I'd keel over. Was n't it warm?"

"I should say yes."

Then there followed some more commonplace remarks about the weather, and at the first opportunity Artie suggested taking a walk.

While Mamie was in the house putting on her hat Artie said: "You 've got lots o' kids up this way."

"The German family in the next house has nine," replied Mrs. Carroll. "If father could 'a' caught one o' them towheaded young 'uns this morning there'd only been eight left. The boy built a bonfire right up against our fence."

"He could run too fast for me," said Mr. Carroll. "Oh, but he's a terror. We have some great youngsters around here. Do you want to get by me, Mamie? Look at the new hat on her."

Artie laughed and Mamie gave her father a playful slap on the arm.

"It's a hun," remarked Artie.

As he followed Mamie down the steps and away toward the corner he somehow felt, because of the silence behind, that Mr. and Mrs. Carroll were watching him and asking themselves whether he was what he pretended to be. On more than one occasion they had shown a liking for him. Certainly they had trusted him. He realized keenly, and for the first time, that they had been kind to him beyond anything he deserved, and with this realization came the resolve that he would never do anything to cause them to change their opinions.

"I'm afraid the old folks'll think we're givin' 'em the shake," said he, as Mamie slipped her arm within his.

"No, no. They do n't mind."

"I guess they're wise enough to tumble to it that I do n't come rubberin' around this neighborhood every two or three nights just to see *them*."

Mamie laughed and put an added pressure on his arm. The gas-lights leaped into balls of flame and Artie felt himself rising into the air. What more could he ask? And yet, as they passed the corner, he was beaming foolishly and had lost his voice.

He had something to tell Mamie — something which would be significant; something to warn her of the supreme question and prepare her for it.

They had come into the business street, where the trolley cars ran and the light was plentiful.

"A little more weather like this and we'll be hittin' the park," he observed.

"I'll be glad," she replied.

They walked in silence for few moments and then he said: "Mame, I've got some good news."

"For me?"

"Well, I s'pose — you may be glad to hear it."

"What is it?"

"I got a boost in my pay."

"Oh, that's lovely."

"I'm gettin' twenty a week now."

"Now I'm jealous. All I get is eight."

"Say, Mame, I'm sore to see you workin' at all."

"I had to do something when I got out of school, and they did n't need me around the house. I would n't mind it if I had a nicer man to work for."

"Who is the main guy up at your place — the pie-face I spoke to the day I come up to see you?"

"Yes, that's him."

"I got it in good and hard for them fellows. Do you know, Mame, this town's full of a lot o' two-by-four dubs that's got into purty fair jobs and it's made 'em so swelled up that you want to take a crack at one of 'em the minute you see him. I'll bet that guy up in your place do n't know nothin' on earth except how to hold down his measly job, and he got that doin' all the mean work around the place. It does me lots o' good to call one o' them proud boys down. If I ever go up there again and he makes any funny play at me I'll come back at him so strong that he won't know what landed on him. Them fellows is counterfeits. They have to put on a horrible front so as to cover up what they do n't

THE PRESIDENT

know. I never see one o' them fellows yet that was n't a four-flush. Take a guy that bellers at kids and bluffs women and put him up against a man of his own weight and he's a cur. If I ever put my hands against that fellow he'd run clear to the roof to get away."

Mame laughed and said: "You've got him sized up just right."

"I'm workin' for a square fellow," continued Artie. "He's *all* right. I used to give him all kinds o' hot and cold roasts, but since he went to the front for me and got my salary whooped I've got to be with him. I'll tell you, Mame, he's this kind. If you'd go up to Morton to-morrow and say: 'How about it; can you take hold and run the earth for a year?' he'd put on one o' them dead easy smiles and say he could do it without turnin' a hair. He's got the nerve to tackle anything. He do n't know nothin', but he do n't need to as long as he can make suckers think he's all right. There's Miller I've told you so much about. He knows more about the business than Morton ever wanted to know, but Morton draws more stuff just because Miller ain't got the face. So I've got wise to this fact: No matter what you've got in your hand play it as if you had a royal flush for a bosom holdout. I weaken on no proposition. If they wanted me to be president o' the whole shootin' match, I'd jump in, grow some side-whiskers and put up as tall a con game as that old stiff we've got down there now. His office hours is from 11:00 to 11:30 and he ain't nothin' but a ham-rester when he *is* there."

Artie had become warmed up, and was walking fast. They stopped at a corner to allow a drove of bicyclers to pass by, and Artie saw the red globes of a drugstore across the street.

"Let's have some o' the cold stuff, Mame," said he, and he led her over to the place.

"Give the lady some strawberry because it's red," said he to the clerk.

"No, you'll not," said she. "I want chocolate ice cream."

"Well, professor, you can make mine the same. Be a good fellow, too, when it comes to droppin' in the ice cream."

"Oh, we put in good measure," said the red-headed boy, as he dug into the freezer.

"That's right. I think you'll do a nice little business on this corner."

XV

"I do n't know about this, Artie," said Miller, as they alighted from the trolley car. "I have no business coming out here with you."

"There you go again!" exclaimed Artie. "Ain't I told you that anybody I bring stands ace-high? W'y, I've been toutin' you to Mame till she's dead crazy to see you. Do n't go to weak'nin' on me at this stage o' the game. You're just as welcome there as you are in the street."

"I dare say," replied Miller, with a nervous little laugh, "but I think you'll have to do most of the talking."

"Let go of that, too. You won't get no frozen face at this place that I'm steerin' you against. Just cut loose the same as if you was at home. I guess you ain't goin' to find no cracked ice in the chairs, and, as I've told you time and again, this girl ain't stuck on frills. She comes purty near bein' able to size up a guy for what he's worth, and you and her'll get along all right."

Notwithstanding these hopeful assurances, Miller was decidedly nervous as they approached the Carroll house. It was only after much persuasion on the part of Artie that he had been induced to come along and now that they were so near the place his apprehensions grew. Miller knew a great deal, but he had never learned how to keep down his pulse and temperature when he was in the presence of a young woman.

"Remember," said Artie, as he preceded Miller up the steps. "Do n't be leary about cuttin' in. Just play you owned the house."

Mamie opened the door and said: "Hello, there," and then, when she saw that Artie was not alone, she gave a small and startled "Oh!"

"Peel your coat and put it any old place," said Artie to Miller.

"Why, Artie," said she, reprovingly.

They were detained in the hallway for a few moments. Artie felt that perhaps he should have presented Miller at the moment of entering, but he preferred to wait until they reached the front room, where there was a full sweep of space at his command.

The critical moment having arrived, Mamie having retreated until she stood beneath the chandelier and Miller having come in from the hall and placed himself, stolid and upright, beside one of the plush chairs, Artie said: "Mame, I want you to shake hands with my friend Mr. Miller, the best ever. Miller, this is little Mame, the girl that makes 'em open all the windows to look at her when she goes along the street."

"I'm so glad to meet you, Mr. Miller," said Mamie. "I've heard so much about you."

She extended her hand and as Miller grasped it and mumbled something, Artie very facetiously remarked, "Take your corners."

Now, if this was his plan for causing Miller to feel perfectly at home, it was not an entire success. Miller laughed rather awkwardly and backed into a chair, where he sat and smiled in a fixed and helpless condition until Mamie came to his rescue.

"I suppose you've learned by this time that you must n't pay any attention to what Artie says," she began. "He does n't mean half he says."

"Here! How about this?" interrupted Artie. "You ain't goin' to begin knockin' the first thing. Pay no attention to what she says about me, Miller. Just copper it. I think she's got her roastin' clothes on to-night."

"I'm afraid I'll have to believe a good many things that he has told me about you," said Miller, with an effort.

"What has he been telling you?"

"Slow up there a little. Be careful," said Artie.

"He said a great many complimentary things about you," persisted Miller.

"Who, me?" demanded Artie. "What are you tryin' to do — string the poor girl? All I ever told you about Mame was the time she shook me for that Indian. I'll tell you about her, Miller. I'm good old car-fare and show-tickets when there's nobody playin' against me, but as soon as any other guy gets in the game she puts me off on the sub bench. I ain't in the play at all. You're here to-night. Am I in it? Well, I should say nit."

Miller laughed good-naturedly and Mamie passed off into an attack of giggles from which she could not easily recover.

"You do n't expect me to pay much attention to you when there's any one else around, do you?" she asked with the merest suggestion of a wink at Miller.

"Certainly not. I'm supposed to be playin' a thinkin' part tonight. I ain't really in the cast at all. I think I come on with a spear in the third act."

"You've heard him talk like that before, have n't you?" asked Mamie of Miller.

"Oh, yes; I've become accustomed to it"

"Oh, what a swipe?" exclaimed Artie. "I think I'll have to lay quiet for awhile after that. What are you doin', Miller; turnin' against me — takin' her part?"

"My goodness, Artie, what did he say that was n't all right?" asked Mamie.

"There you are, Miller. She's huntin' a scrap because I spoke cross to you. I told you I would n't be in it after I brought you up here."

"Artie, I want you to behave. I'm going to ask Mr. Miller all about how you carry on at the office."

"Oh, his conduct is very good," Miller hastened to say.

"That's what you boys always say about each other. Does he ever work?"

"Do I ever work!" Artie interrupted. "Do you think I could travel on my shape? She ought to see us doin' the slave act there the first of every month; eh, Miller?"

"We have to work hard enough," said Miller.

"He's told me all this," said Mamie; "but he 'kids' so much, as he call it, that I do n't know when he's telling the truth and when he is n't. Why, do you know, Mr. Miller, the first time I met him, he told me his name was something-or-other and that he was on the Board of Trade — oh, the worst string of stuff you ever heard."

Miller had to laugh, because he had already been told the whole story by Artie.

"Did you believe it?" he asked.

"Believe it? I should say not. He told me the worst whoppers you ever heard about how much money he made and lost on the Board of Trade. What's more, just to show you the cheek of that boy, the fellow that he had come over and introduce him I never saw before in all my life."

Miller had to laugh in earnest. Artie had told him the same story, but had claimed that Mamie believed everything she heard.

For once Artie was red, embarrassed and at a loss to reply. He smiled feebly when Miller laughed, and then he managed to say: "I guess you waged up some purty good fairy yarns yourself that night."

"I was trying to keep up with you," said Mamie, gaily.

Artie's grin widened and he glanced significantly at Miller.

"What did I tell you?" he asked. "Ain't she a child wonder?"

And by that time Miller was well enough acquainted to join in and talk on many topics.

It was after ten o'clock when they left the house and started for the car.

"Well, will she do?" asked Artie almost as soon as the door had closed behind them.

"Yes, indeed," replied Miller, warmly. "She's an awfully nice girl."

"Nothin' mushy, eh? None o' this soft work?"

"No, sir. She's a good, sensible girl."

"How about her bein' a good looker?"

"Artie, you may think I'm trying to flatter you, but really she is a very pretty girl — very pretty."

"Say, I tumbled that she was the real stuff the first time I ever see her. You got next to how she give me that horrible jolt about the dance, did n't you?"

"I should say so."

"Now, there's a wise girl. She knew awful well that I'd told you about meetin' her at the dance, and how I caught her that night, and she just brought the thing up to square herself with you. She did n't want you to think that any Reub could go up and flag her."

"Oh, well, you can see that she is n't that kind of a girl."

"Sure. They do n't grow 'em on the Lake Shore drive any better behaved than she is now."

XVI

Every breeze that came in at the open windows was as soft as velvet. The warm sunshine had tempered it until the last sting of winter was gone.

Miller and Artie had removed their coats and unbuttoned their vests. They worked listlessly, and occasionally one of them would lean back and gaze sleepily out at the walls and roofs and the distant ribbon of lake, now dotted here and there with moving specks.

"A man ought to be pinched for workin' a day like this," Artie finally observed.

"Is n't it delightful?" said Miller. "This is the time of year when a man feels like getting out into the country."

"That ain't no lie, neither. You do n't see very many Johnny-jump-ups growin' along Dearborn street, do you?"

"Do you expect to get away from town often this summer?"

"Gee, I can't go very far. Since I've started plantin' my stuff in the bank and plunkin' in a few cases every month on the buildin' and loan game, I've got to play purty close to my bosom, I'll tell you those. Night before last, though, I was fixin' it up with Mame to take a little run over to St. Joe or up to Milwaukee on the boat. When they let you ride all day on the boat for a dollar a throw, w'y, that's where I cut in freely. But they do n't get my game at any o' them summer resorts where they set you back five big elegant bucks a day for a room about as big as that telephone box over there. Then if you want anything to chew you've got to square the waiter every time you go in the dinin'-room. I went up against one o' them places last summer. I commenced owin' money to that hotel before I got off the train. They cleaned me in two days, but then, as they say down on State street, I was n't very dirty when I landed."

"If I'm going to take a vacation," said Miller, "I'd rather get right out into the country. Do n't you like the country?"

"Well, I ain't dead sure about that. I 'spose the country's all right to a man that's lived there, but you take some wise boy that was brought up in town, and you throw him out on a farm, and he's the worst ever. You've seen them boys around the Union station comin' in with their red-topped boots and high hats and paper grips — well, when you see them fallin' into coal-holes and bein' snaked out by fake hotel-runners you think they're purty new, do n't you? Well, say, there ain't one o' them that's half the horrible mark that some Chicago dub is when he goes up against that farm game. If he do n't look like a yellow clarinet in twenty-four hours you can mark me down for a sucker. They can't spring none o' that happy-childhood-days-down-on-the-farm business on me. I've been next, I'll tell you those."

"I did n't know that you were ever on a farm," said Miller, laughing.

"I was there once, all right, and I got it throwed into me so hard I was good and sore, too. Four years ago this summer — that was before my father died — my uncle Matt, that's got a farm a little ways from Galesburg, wrote for me to come down and visit 'em. The old gentleman asked me if I wanted to go, and I said, 'Sure thing; in a minute.' I'd been readin' them con story-books about pickin' flowers and goin' fishin' and dubbin' around the woods out in the country, and I thinks to myself: 'This is a cinch. I'll go down there and dazzle them jays.' So I went down there, and a cousin 'o mine, Spencer Blanchard, met me at the train with a buggy and drove me out. I got there in time for supper, and they all give me the glad hand and jollied me up, and I kind o' thought that first night that I'd be a warm proposition out there. Well, holy smoke! about the time they got the dishes washed up the uncle says to me, 'I guess we'd better turn in.' 'What do you mean?' I says; 'go to bed?' 'Sure thing,' says he. 'We got to get all kinds of an early start in the morning.' I could n't stand for that. I put up a holler right at the jump. I told 'em I was just usually beginnin' to enjoy myself about nine o'clock in the evening. They said I could set up if I wanted to, and then they ducked and turned in. Well, I did n't want to turn in, but there was nothin' to keep me up. I set out by the pump for a little while smokin' and listenin' to them katydids gettin' in their work, and then I went in the house and went to bed, but I could n't get to sleep before midnight. It seemed to me I'd been poundin' my ear about ten minutes when somebody walloped me in the back and hollered, 'Get up.' Well, I set up in bed, and — honest, Miller, this ain't no kid — it was dark outside. 'What's the trouble?' I says. 'Is the house on fire?' It was my cousin Spencer that give me the jolt in the back. 'It's time to get up,' he says. I asked him what time it was, and what do you think he said? This is on the level, too. He says, 'It's past four.' When he said that I did n't know what kind of a combination I'd struck."

"I guess people in the country often get up that early in the summer time, especially in the busy season," said Miller.

"They'd never got me up, I tell you those, only that fresh cousin o' mine grabbed me by the leg and pulled me out. Oh, he's a playful guy, all right. Well, I put on my clothes and went downstairs, dead on my feet. You see, I was shy four or five hours' sleep. When they see me they all give me the horse-laugh, even the hired girl. My aunt asked me what time I got up when I was in town, and I said never before seven o'clock, and then they all yelled again. They seemed to think I was wrong in my nut out there. Everything I done or said they give me the ha-ha."

"Of course life in the city is much different," said Miller.

"Well, I guess yes. I know this town like a book. I can begin at the first card and go through the deck, but out there — they lose me. They had me lookin' like a Reub all the time. The worst one was the hired hand. His name was Elias. I see him up here the time of the World's Fair, dodgin' cable cars and lookin' up at the skyscrapers. He was dead lucky to get out o' town without havin' his clothes lifted, and, at that, I ain't sure he did. But down at the farm, he was the wise guy and I was the soft mark. What do you think? The second day I was there I goes out in the field where they was cuttin' down the oats with one o' them bindin' machines, and 'Lias asked me to go back to the barn and ask Uncle Matt if he had a left-handed monkey wrench. How was I to know? I ain't up on monkey-wrenches. Gee, I went drillin' way back to the barn through the hot sun, and when I sprung the left-handed monkey-wrench on the uncle it made a horrible hit with him. He hollered around till I got kind o' sore. Then he went in the house and told them and they all had a fit about it. But you ought o' seen 'Lias when he come in at night. He was all swelled up over the way he throwed it into me. He thought he was a better comedian than Nat Goodwin. He must a' gone for two miles all around tellin' that monkey-wrench story, and a lot o' the hands used to come over and kid me. They'd laugh and slap their legs and say, 'By Jing!' They had me crazy. I used to think it was n't on the square to josh a man because he was from the country, but do n't you fool yourself — them country people won't do a thing to a city guy if they ever get him out where they can take a good, fair crack at him."

"It was all in fun, though, was n't it?" asked Miller.

"Oh, sure; they thought they was givin' me a good time. There was a kid cousin o' mine, Rutherford Hayes Blanchard — would n't that name frost you? — that jollied me into ridin' bareback on one o' the old pelters they had around the place. I was up in the air most o' the time, and after I got through ridin' mebbe you think I was n't sore. This same kid took me down to the crick to go swimmin'. I burned the skin off o' my back, got a peach of a stone bruise on my foot, and while I was in, 'Lias and Spencer come over and tied my clothes in hard knots. That's just a sample. Oh, I had a nice time. After a day or two I shook my town clothes and made up for a farmer but I couldn't play the part. They used to make me try to hitch up the team without anyone helpin', and then they'd all stand around and kid me when I made bad breaks. It was a cinch that I'd fall down. I did n't know a whiffle-tree from a tug. Then they had me milkin', too. I do n't know whether you're on to it or not, but if you try to play up to a cow on the wrong side of her she's liable to make a sassy pass and land the knockout. Well, the first night they took me out to milk they steered me up against the bum side o' the cow. I'm purty game myself, an' I did n't want to quit, but she was too good for me. She kept me busy for about five minutes, and then I went to my corner and said I had enough. Say, the whole push had been leanin' on the fence laughin' at me till they cried. I guess they had more fun around that place while I was there than they ever had before. I stood it for about ten days, helpin' em' work in the fields, gettin' all tanned up and roundin' in to supper every night smellin' like a laundry, and then I kind o' figured it out that farm life was too swift for me. I kind o' wanted to see the 'lectric lights and the tall houses again. So I said I was goin'. They made an awful kick for me to stay. They knew they had a good thing. But I broke away."

"Then you're not fond of the country?"

"It's this way. I would n't mind goin' out for awhile if I could play myself off as company, but when it comes to bein' one of the family — nit, nit."

XVII

"Well, I'm goin' to be one o' them boys," said Artie, after he had seated himself and turned half-way around so that he could see Miller.

"What boys?" asked Miller.

"Them bike people with the fried-egg caps and the wall-paper stockins'. I'm goin' to be the sassiest club boy in the whole push. You just wait. In about a week I'll come hot-footin' in here with my knee-pants and a dinky coat, and do the club yell."

"I knew you'd get it sooner or later."

"This thing got the half-Nelson on me before I know it. One night I goes to bed feelin' all right and the next mornin' when I woke up I was wrong. There was somethin' ailed me, but I was n't wise to it. The first thing I know I was stoppin' along the street lookin' at the wheels in the windows and gettin' next to the new kinds o' saddles and rubber-neckin' to read the names on the tires, and all that business. Then I begin to see that I had it the same as everybody else."

"I noticed that you'd been talking bicycle lately, but I did n't know you were going to get one."

"I'll tell you. I had a spiel with Mame last night and we fixed it up that if we did n't ride wheels this summer we would n't be in it at all, so I'm goin' to do the sucker act and blow myself."

"Does Mamie ride?"

"Does she? She's a scorchalorum. You ought o' seen her pushin' around the block last night on the Connelly girl's wheel. I told her if she ever went through the park speedin' like that she'd have all the sparrow cops layin' for her."

"How did she learn if she has n't a wheel?"

"Just picked it up. Ain't I told you she's a world-beater? She's got the dough saved up to buy a wheel, too. There's a funny thing.

A girl has to work for nothin', but she can always keep herself dressed right and show a little bank roll to the good. A man gets two or three times as much coin — always on the hog, and goin' around lookin' like a tramp. If Mame had my salary she'd be collectin' rent on flat buildin's."

"What kind of a wheel are you going to get?"

"Now you've got me guessin'. I've talked to twenty wise guys that've been ridin,' and every one of 'em sings a different song. Every guy cracks up his own wheel, and says all the others is made out o' sheet iron and bum castin's. I've had five or six chances to get inside prices. A friend o' mine fixed it so I can get a purty fair wheel for fifty and pay for it at five a week, and I think I'll take it."

"Can you ride?"

"I can stay on, but when it comes to stickin' to a straight line or turnin' around to come back I'm purty tart. The only practice I've had is on some o' the wheels that belong to the boys out at the boathouse. Anybody that gets on the same street with me is takin' horrible chances. I never know what I'm goin' to carom against. The other day I tried to climb a lamp-post and a lot of fresh kids stood around and give me the laugh."

"How does it happen that you never wanted a wheel before? I've been riding for two years."

"There was too many Charley-boys ridin'. You know the kind I mean — them dubs with the long hair and the badges all over the coats. W'y I've seen 'em with tobacco tags, campaign buttons and little ribbons hung all over the front of 'em. I could n't stand for nothin' like that. They was out just to make a show o' themselves. This year it's different. Everybody's gone nutty on the proposition. You can go out on a bike now without every driver tryin' to upset you and all the people joshin' you about your knee-pants."

"It's wonderful, the number of people riding wheels this spring," said Miller.

"I'll tell you they've gone daffy and I'm one of 'em. I'm goin' to be the worst fan in the whole bunch. What do you think last Sunday out at Lincoln Park? Old geezers — ye-e-s, the white-haired boys that you'd think was too stiff to back a wheel out of a shed, they was out there in them dizzy togs cuttin' up and down the

MAMIE'S MOTHER

track like two-year-olds. And old girls, too — girls from away back, about the crop o' '45 — fat ones, too — poundin' the pedals and duckin' in and out past the rigs! W'y, when I see it I put both hands in the air and I says: 'Well, when the old people can cut in on this game it's about time for me to begin to associate.' I'll be with 'em, too, next Sunday."

"Are you going to wear a suit?" asked Miller.

"Well, I'm a little leary on that. I do n't want to get too gay on the jump. Mame wants me to get one and be right in line with all them club boys, but when she first sprung it on me I said: 'Nix; if I ever come up here with one o' them funny suits on the old man might take a shot at me.' Here's a funny thing about that. Here's somethin' that'll knock you cold. Last night when I gets to the house to see the girl, Mrs. Carroll's on the front porch and I could see she was hot about something. I asked her if anything had gone wrong and she says, 'Mr. Blanchard, there's an old man around the corner makin' a fool of himself. If you've got any drag with him I wish you'd go and get him in the house before he breaks his neck.' I was n't on to what she was talkin' about, but she pointed to the corner and I walked over there and say — this a good thing — if there was n't Mame's old man takin' a fall out of a wheel. He'd borrowed it from one o' the neighbors, and this guy was holdin' him on and jollyin' him along. 'Do n't be afraid,' he says, 'you won't fall.' The old man's eyes was hangin' out, and he was workin' them handle-bars like a man twistin' a brake. Gee, he was a sight. I had to holler and then he looked up and saw me. Course that rattled him and over he went. He made a fair fall, too, both shoulders on the ground and Mr. Bike on top of him. You ought o' heard some o' the large blue language the old man got rid of soon as we took the wheel off of him. I did n't know it was in him. 'Try it again,' this neighbor says and he was takin' long chances on gettin' his wheel smashed at that. But the old man would n't listen to it. He went limpin' back to the house, and Mrs. Carroll says: 'Well, I hope you're satisfied now.' The old man give her the cold eye, and then he says to me: 'She'd talk that way if I'd been killed.' I guess Mame's mother is the only people on the North Side that ain't monkeyin' with a wheel."

"When do you and Mamie make your first appearance?"

"As soon as we can get the wheels. If I do n't get mine inside of a week I'll go bug-house. I'm dreamin' wheels, I tell you. Last night I dreamt I was goin' along at about forty miles an hour and run into a steam roller."

"Did it break the wheel?"

"I give it up. I woke up and found myself tryin' to get the strangle hold on the pillow."

"Is Mamie going to wear bloomers?"

"Is she? Is she goin' to wear 'em — bloomers? Not on your facial expression. The first time we talked wheel I got up and declared myself on the bloomer business. I done the tall talk. I told her any time she sprung them Turkish village clothes on her Artie boy, all bets was goin' to be declared off."

"Why, what's the matter? Bloomers are all right."

"They're all right on some other guy's girl, but they do n't go in my set. When I see my girl come on a wheel I want to know whether it's her or some Board o' Trade clerk. I do n't want to be kept guessin'."

"Why, what's wrong with bloomers?"

"I'll tell you. The first one I ever see in bloomers was a lemon-faced fairy that ought o' been picked along about centennial year. She come peltin' along Michigan avenue with one o' them ballet-girl smiles splittin' that face o' hers, and I aint kiddin' when I tell you that a horse jumped up on the sidewalk and tried to get in the Risholoo hotel so as to pass it up. For a month afterwards I'd see that face at night and I'd wake up and holler: "Take it away!' From the minute I see this good thing on Michigan I'm dead sore on all bloomers. I never see a good-lookin' girl wear 'em yet. Some of 'em might have been good lookers before they got into 'em but after that — nit. You need n't be afraid o' Mame, and what's more, I do n't want to talk about her wearin' them things at all. I like her too well. Do you think I'm goin' out ridin' with her and have a lot o' cheap skates stoppin' to play horse with her everywhere we go? Not in a thousand years. Besides, she do n't have to make up like a man to make people look at her. She ain't like some o' the others. W'y, she kills 'em dead in her street clothes. Bloomers! Well, if Mame goes with me she goes as a girl, and that ain't no lie, neither."

XVIII

As Artie came in he saw a stranger seated near Miller's desk. The stranger was rather well dressed, although his garments were not of the latest cut. He had a good tan color in his face, and for that and some other reasons which he could not have explained to himself, Artie knew that the stranger was merely a visitor to Chicago.

"O Artie," said Miller, "I want you to meet my cousin, Walter Miller. He lives in my old town. Walter, this is Mr. Blanchard, Artie Blanchard."

"He was just speaking about you," said the cousin, with an amiable but rather embarrassed smile.

"Did he gi' me the worst of it?" inquired Artie. "I s'pose he did. He's on to the story of my past life."

"No," said Miller. "I was just telling him that if he wanted to know anything about Chicago you were the man that could tell him."

"Well, that's a good send off. What are you doin'? Passin' me off as one o' the sights o' the town? I s'pose you told him that every visitor to Chicago ought to see Lincoln Park, the stockyards, the sky-scrapers and Artie Blanchard and then buy a box o' candy for the loved ones at home."

"No, but I told him you were just as good as a guide-book."

"Better. I can put him next to things that ain't in the guide-books. Come over here next to the window where there's a draught, Mr. Miller. You might as well take the air freely. That's the only thing in Chicago that you'll get for nothin'."

"I believe you're about right," remarked the cousin, as he moved over to a place near the window. "Coming up the street this morning I wanted a glass of water, and I finally had to go into a saloon and buy it."

"If you'd had a beer thirst you'd have been all right. Is this the first time you've been up against the town?"

"No, I was here a week the time of the World's Fair, but I did n't get into this part of town much."

"Well, what do you think of it as far as you've got? Warm town, eh?"

"Yes, indeed; wonderful. I always feel rather lost when I get in the crowds."

"I s'pose it is that way for a day or two, but you'd soon get used to it."

"I do n't believe I would. There are too many people here. I'm afraid I'd never get along in Chicago."

"You want to get over that in a hurry. Of course there's an awful push in the streets here any day, and I s'pose when you first get in you kind o' feel that you're up against a lot o' wise city mugs and that they must be purty fly because they live right here in town. I've had people tell me that's the way they felt at first, but it did n't take 'em long to find out there's just as many pin-heads on State street as you'll find anywhere out in the woods."

"Oh, I suppose a man would learn about the city in a little while?"

"Cert. It ain't where a man's born or where he was raised that puts him in any class. It's whether he's got anything under his hat. I seen too many o' these boys kind o' jump in from the country and make a lot o' city boys look like rabbits. You see, Mr. Miller, when a guy comes in from the country he figures it out: 'Here, I'm goin' against a tough proposition, and I've got to hump myself to keep up.' He's willin' to learn a few things and do the best he can. If he feels that way he stands to win out. But if he comes canterin' into town to be a dead-game sport and set a pace for all the boys, w'y, he do n't last. It's a small town, but it's too big for any one boy to come in from the country and scare it. Then sporty boys do n't last. They get in with a lot o' cheap skates and chase around at nights and think they're the real thing, and then in a couple o' moons they go back home and leave all their stuff in hock. They think they're fly, but they ain't."

"I know some that have done that very thing."

"Sure you do. I ain't roastin' no man 'cause he's from the country.

You go along Prairie avenue and see all o' them swell joints where the fat boys with side-whiskers hang out. Well, them boys all come in from the country, but they had sense enough to saw wood and plant a little coin when it begin to come easy. I'm tellin' you, the worst suckers you'll find is some o' these city people that know it all to begin with. They got such a long start on everybody else that they do n't need to learn nothin'. If they know the names o' the streets, what shows is in town next week, what color of a necktie to flash and what was the score at the ball game they think they come purt' near bein' dead wise. You live here in town awhile and you'll get on to them people. Say! I know a lot o' boys that's got just enough sense to put in workin' hours and then go ridin' a wheel. You could n't set 'em down and tell 'em a thing. Any of 'em that's got himself staked to a spring suit and knows the chorus o' 'Paradise Alley' thinks he's up to the limit. You can make book that them boys'll be workin' on bum salaries when they're gray headed, and what's more, they'll be workin' for some Reub that come into town wearin' hand-me-downs."

"Well, I suppose folks out in the country do give the city people too much credit for being smart," said the visitor.

"Oh, we've got 'em smart enough, all right, all right, but I'm tellin' you about the cheap ones. You're a stranger here and you see some guy goin' along State street puttin' on a horrible front, tryin' to kill women right and left, a big piece o' rock salt on his necktie, and you say, 'Hully gee, I wonder who that case o' swell is; Marshall Field or P. D. Armour?' Well, say, it's a ten to one shot that all that that fellow's got in the world he's got right with him, and at that it ain't no cinch he's wearin' underclothes. You've got to learn these things. You don't know — mebbe that guy can't spell through the first reader. Any old farmer with one o' them bunches on his chin could buy up him and a hundred more like him. Well, he's just the kind of a counterfeit that'd go out in the country and play himself off as the real boy because he lives in the city. Now, do n't you fool yourself for a minute, Mr. Miller. Take my tip. We've got just as many suckers up here as you've got down your way."

"I think you're right about that," said Miller, who had been listening.

"You know it. Take them mashers along State street. Can you beat 'em anywhere? Then a little farther south you'll see them stranded boys, goin' around on their uppers and takin' a dip at the free lunch when nobody's lookin'. They'd sooner stand around in town and starve to death than get out somewhere and make a stand for the coin. Any one o' them vags thinks he's too good to go out in the country or to some little town and live decent."

"It's tough down that way. I walked up through there this morning," said the visiting Miller.

"You can get any kind of a game you want down there, but you're safe if you do n't go huntin' trouble. Any man that keeps hot-footin' right along and says nothin' to nobody is all right. Of course, when one of these new boys comes in and raps on the bar and says he's got money to burn there's always some handy man right there to give him a match. When that kind of a mark comes in they get out the bottle o' knock-out drops and get ready to do business. A man like you, Mr. Miller, won't have no trouble here. And for goodness sake do n't think you're up against anything great when you're minglin' with Chicago people. When you come to know the town it's as common as plowed ground. I know a good show I'll take you to to-night."

XIX

It was Saturday morning and Artie came in wearing his bicycle clothes.

"How do you like 'em?" he asked, turning about so that Miller and young Mr. Hall could see the hang of the coat. "Reduced from nineteen bones to seven seventy-five. Are you next to the stockin's? I guess I ain't got no shape or nothin'."

"It looks first rate on you," said young Mr. Hall.

"Well, why not, why not? I think I'm one o' the purtiest boys that works here in the office — anyway, that's what a good many people tell me."

"You did n't have it made, did you?" asked Miller.

"Aw, let go; do n't ask such questions. Do n't it look just as good as if I'd coughed up twenty-five plunks for it, huh?"

"It's a dressy suit," said Miller. "But why are you wearing it this morning?"

"W'y, the minute I get through here I'm goin' out to meet the girl, and we're goin' over to the park just to show people the difference."

"You're still going out to see that girl, are you?" asked young Mr. Hall.

"My boy, you're very slow here lately. You've been overlookin' a lot o' news."

"You had n't told me anything about her for a long time."

"That's because she ain't been sendin' any word to you. Miller's been out to see her."

"Have you, Miller?" inquired young Mr. Hall.

"Of course — had a good time."

"When you're a little older — if you're good — I'll take you out some night and let you meet some o' the real folks."

"Oh, thanks," said young Mr. Hall, with a little twitch, suggestive of sarcasm, at one corner of his mouth. "Do you think you could introduce me to society."

"I could take you where you'd have to shake that Miss Maud business and comb your hair different or else go to the wall. If you ever went out to the Carrolls and sprung that gum-drop talk the old man wouldn't do a thing to you."

"It must be a pleasant sort of place," said young Mr. Hall, who had flushed up at the reference to the "Miss Maud business."

"The best ever — if you belong."

Young Mr. Hall smiled complacently and said: "Now I know why you've changed so much lately. I kind of believed you were still stuck on the girl."

"Who's changed? What are you talkin' about?"

"Why, you have. I've noticed you never chew tobacco any more for one thing. Did she make you stop?"

"No, she did n't. Well you've got a rind, ain't you? What if she had? What's it to you?"

"Nothing, only I can notice the change. You do n't cuss like you used to, nor smoke as much, and I've seen you writing letters on that square paper and looking out of the window with the funniest kind of a look——"

"Break away! Say, I believe you're tryin' to kid me. You talk like a man that was full of dope."

"I'll leave it to Miller," persisted young Mr. Hall. "Has n't he changed, Miller? Gracious me, I could notice it. I didn't know what the reason was, because after that first time he never told me anything about this."

"Oh, get tired, can't you!" interrupted Artie. "You must think you're good if you can string me."

"I'll leave it to Miller," repeated young Mr. Hall.

"Well," said Miller, laughing, "of course Artie has changed some, but——"

"There!" exclaimed young Mr. Hall, triumphantly.

"Humph!" said Artie. His face was red and he was certainly flustered. "It'd be a dead lucky thing if some more people around the shop'd change a little. They could n't be any punker'n they are now."

DIFFERENT

But young Mr. Hall did not retort. He had made his point and was satisfied.

A few moments later young Mr. Hall put on his hat and started away on his daily round of collections. Artie turned from his desk and said to Miller: "Say, that boy kind o' had me down on the mat, did n't he?"

"Do n't mind what he says."

"Yes, but he had the best of it. I did n't s'pose he'd noticed I was goin' queer. They say a man never does know it when he goes off the jump. On the level, though, he's dead right. I ain't like I was the first time I met the girl. No more chasin' around at nights, no blowin' my stuff against a lot o' dubs and no more boozin'."

"I'd noticed that."

"Sure. I ain't had a package since that night I told you about, and then they made me take it."

"Package? What's that?"

"W'y, a load, a jag! Smoke up! Do n't go out on me. You ought to know what a package is."

"I never had one."

"Well, I've had 'em when I had to lay down in the grass and hold on with both hands to keep from fallin' off the earth. I've had 'em when I made tracks like a man drivin' geese. I was like lots more o' them sporty boys — wanted to throw in the big bowls just to show I was nice people. There ain't a thing in it. Most o' them West Side boys I started in to train with got to be dead tough. I do n't want to star myself, but I think I had enough wiseness to switch. I ain't no blue-ribbon boy, but if you ever see little old Artie with a load o' peaches you can just take him and drop him in the river and say: 'Here goes nothin'.'"

"There's nothing like a good, sensible girl to straighten a fellow up."

"Mebbe that ain't no lie, neither. She ain't never struck me to do nothin', but I just says: 'Here, you big mark, if you're goin' to be around with a nice girl, why, you 've got to be nice people.' If there's anything that makes me sore it's to see some swell-lookin' girl goin' around with a guy actin' like a Reub or a dead tough. If he done his best, you know, he could n't belong with her. If I do say it myself, I've used Mame the best I know how and been purty square. Of course a man livin' in this Indian village may think he's on the square as long as he keeps out o' the cooler, but I know I ain't been as tough as a lot more. What knocks me is to think this mamma's boy got on to me. I must be gettin' purty far along when that guy gets next and tries to play horse with me. Everybody must be on. I s'pose them elevator boys is sayin'; 'Well, about day after to-morrow they'll put his nobs into cell 13 and send for the doctors.'"

"Nonsense, nonsense," said Miller, laughing in spite of himself. "You're all right. I wish I was stuck on some girl. Then I'd know what to do evenings."

"Evenings! Say, Miller, there ought to be about ten evenings every week. If things keep on the way they've been since both of us went daffy on the bike game, I'll have to give up my job here and move Mr. Trunk up to the Carroll joint. I'm gettin' too busy to work. My job's been interferin' with me a good deal lately. I'd give it up only for one thing."

"What's that?"

"W'y, the dough, of course. You will have to smoke up, sure enough. Now I think I'll do a little work so as to get through early. Mame and me want to do a century by 4 o'clock. I went eighteen miles before breakfast this morning. I may be a sloppy rider, but I'm one of the best 150-pound liars in the business."

"Well, get to work," said Miller. "I'm going to be busy myself."

"What are you hurryin' to get through for? You ain't got nothin' in this world to live for. You 're nothin' but a chair-warmer."

"Never you mind. Some day I'll fool you."

"Well, if it happens I'll be fooled all right, all right."

And with that he went to work.

XX

A full moon was hanging over the lake. The whole surface of small, uneasy waves was lighted. There was one path of shiny splendor leading straight out toward the moon and where this path lost itself no one could tell.

"There ain't no moon for nothin' tonight," observed Artie. He had been flipping pebbles down the paved beach and into the water. Mamie sat with him on the stone uplift dividing the park driveway from the slope toward the water — with him, to be sure, but three or four feet away, with her hat in her lap. "It's *perfectly* lovely to-night," she said.

The two bicycles were leaned over against the stone uplift and the lamps threw oblong splotches of light on the gravel.

Behind Artie and Mamie was the gloomy range made by the heavy foliage of the park. In and out amid the dark banks of trees and along the level driveway moved glow specks like so many busy fireflies. Artie saw none of these, for he was intent on the spectacle of water and moonshine.

"The guy that could put all that into a picture' be a bird, eh, Mame?"

"It's *perfectly* lovely."

"That's what it is, all right. They don't grow many like this one."

"I could stay out here all night and just look at the lake."

"Could you? Well, I think about two o'clock in the morning I'd be ready to let go. It *is* a peach of a night, though, I'll say that."

"Sing something, Artie."

"What do you want me to do — drive the moon in? How did you ever come to think I was a singer? That's two or three times you've sprung that on me. Somebody must 'a' been stringin' you."

"Why, the night we walked home from Turner Hall you sang something awfully pretty. What was it?"

"Well, let it go at that. Any singin' I ever done was a horrible bluff, I'll tell you those."

"Oh, you contrary thing! You can sing if you try to."

"I take no chances, Mame. If I'd ever spring one o' them bum notes you'd gi' me the horse laugh and then there'd be trouble."

Mamie laughed and said: "What a boy you are! You never do anything I want you to."

"Come off! I'll tell you right now that when I kick on singin' I'm doin' you the greatest favor in the world. You never heard me sing. I guess you're a little mixed in your dates. It must a' been somebody else you had on your staff that night."

"Why Artie Blanchard, you mean thing!"

"Hello! Did I land on you that time?"

"I think it was awfully mean of you to say that. I don't ever ask you if you've been running around with some other girl."

"Why don't you? I'd tell you there's three or four others that kind o' like my style."

"They must be hard up."

"Is that so? Maybe I ain't so many but I'm a purty good thing, at that. I'm fresh every hour. No family ought to be without me. When you lose me you lose a puddin', and do n't you overlook it."

In answer, Mamie picked up some of the small pebbles and threw them at him. He held his cap over his face and laughingly begged of her to stop.

"Will you be good?" she asked.

"Sure thing. But do n't be so rough with your man."

"My man!" Mamie tilted her head back, looked at the moon and shrieked with laughter.

Artie was always vastly pleased to have Mamie understand his bantering way. He had often wondered if they would ever come to the habit of taking each other seriously. Could married people keep up the joke?

"I seem to be makin' a horrible hit with you to-night," he remarked, as Mamie slowly recovered from the attack.

Mamie looked at him seriously for a moment and again broke into laughter.

"What's the joke?" demanded Artie. "Put me next so I can get in on the laugh."

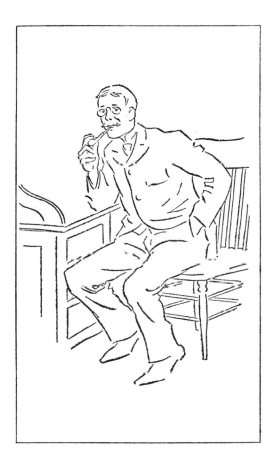

MILLER

"Oh nothing. Only you said that so funny."

"Funny? That was on the level."

At this moment Artie had an inspiration. The conversation was headed right. Why not steer it straight ahead?

"Of course," he continued, "I was kind o' kiddin' when I said that, but when it comes right down to cases it was n't so much of a kid after all."

Mamie laughed a little, but it was a forced laugh. She had suddenly become interested in a pebble which she was rolling under the toe of her shoe.

"I do n't mean more 'n half I say," said Artie, tightening his firsts with resolution and still looking at the illuminated lake, "but on the dead, Mame, I ain't as foolish sometimes as I am others. That talk about there bein' any other girl was all guff."

"Pshaw, I knew that."

"Gee, you know you've got me right, do n't you? And I guess you have, too. That ain't no lie. Say, Mame, what do you think? Miller was roastin' me the other day. He said I was slow."

"Slow — how?"

"About doin' the nervy thing — comin' out and sayin to you, 'Here, let's fix it up.'"

"Fix what up?"

"Oh, you do n't know, do you? You ain't got no notion at all of what I'm gettin' at, have you? That's too bad about you."

Mamie began to laugh and then she checked herself, for she observed that Artie was frowning.

"Of course," she said, "I suppose you mean — that we ——"

'All I mean is, what's the matter of gettin' it settled that it's goin' to be a case of marry?"

There! When he said this it seemed to him that his voice went further and further away from him, as if some one else were speaking the words.

Mamie was smiling quietly and turning her hat over and over.

"I guess that did n't scare you so much after all," said Artie, who at that moment felt that his whole existence had stepped out from under a burden.

"No," she replied, as she continued to fuss with the hat. "Scare me?"

"How about it bein' up to you?"

"Oh, it's all right, I guess." She spoke with a frightened attempt to be careless.

"This is one of them cases where all guessin 's barred."

"Well, you might know it's all right."

"It's a go then."

He said this rather solemnly. There was a pause, then he continued with some embarrassment: "I'll tell you, Mame, it seemed to me we ought to have it through with. I did n't want to keep you guessin' whether I wanted to stick. Do n't you think it was the wise move — huh?"

"It's all right — yes."

"I was goin' to spring it on you sooner, but I ain't never got the nerve to talk much about things like that. It ain't like askin' a girl to go to a show, is it?"

"Not exactly," and then both of them laughed, in a relieved way.

"Do n't you think you'd better put your mother on to it?" asked Artie.

"I do n't know. Would you?"

"Sure. I guess she won't make no holler."

Mamie laughed again. "That's a good one on you," she said.

"What is?"

"She wanted to know the other day if you'd asked me yet."

"Who, the old girl? Well, what do you think of that? Everybody's on to us, Mame."

"I do n't care."

"Care? They can bill the town with it if they want to. Come on; let's take another whirl through the park."

As they walked over to the bicycles Artie laid his hand on her shoulder, much as one man might have put his hand on the shoulder of another man. His voice trembled with what he pretended was laughter as he said: "Mrs. Blanchard, you're the best o' the lot. How's the lamp workin'? Here, I'll turn it up a little."

Perhaps he would have kissed her, as he quakingly felt that he should have done, had they not been standing in the moonlight. Yet he did not know that he was in the temper for love-making. He was simply filled with a large wonder that he had succeeded beyond his deserts and that this one best creature of all time was satisfied with him.

They quickly mounted the wheels and moved northward. The darting specks of fire were still abroad, but there was no sound except that soft rasp of the turning wheels. Artie, pumping leisurely and watching the lighted patch of roadway fleeing before his wheel, suddenly began to sing about "Marguerite." He was singing absent-mindedly and merely to keep time with his thoughts, but Mamie heard him and swung her wheel so as to ride up close beside him.

"I thought you did n't sing," said she, laughing.

"Oh, well," said Artie, grinning. "You know there are times — there are times."

PINK MARSH

On Spending a Million Dollars

He happened into the place one afternoon in the late autumn.
They met by chance — the usual way. If he had shaved himself
that morning, as he should have done, he never would have met
Pink. Perhaps Fate issued a sub-decree.

That afteroon as he moved through the weaving crowd toward
the corner where his trolley-car stopped for him, he felt of his
face and found it stubbled. The shop opened invitingly at the
bottom of a white stairway. Most of the barber-shops in Chicago
are underground. He descended to the shop and sat in the first
chair. When he had been tilted back he closed his eyes so as to
keep away the horrors of a ceiling-design. The conversation, which
had ceased when he entered, was then taken up again.

"I know, but s'pose you *did* find a million dollars. Would n't
you keep it?"

"That depends."

"Don' ask me, Misteh Adams. I would n' keep no million dollahs
faw minute, would I? They'd have to chlo'fohm me to get 'at money
'way f'om me."

"Yes, but then if you give it back to the man that owned it he
might give you as much as twenty thousand dollars."

"Who would? My goodness, misteh white man bahbeh, people
don' get no million dollahs now'days by givin' way money. No,
seh! Huh-uh! It's 'bout fo' to one 'at any man's got as much as
million dollahs ain't goin' 'o open up. Chances is he'd give you
'bout fo' dollahs."

"Yes, but what good would this money do you? If you went to
throwin' a million dollars around do n't you s'pose the police 'd be
onto you? They'd be lookin' for the man that found the money."

"You could n't have that money ten minutes without flashin' it."

"Look heah, I fool you. Do you reckon I'd spend 'at money right away? No, seh! I'd wait 'bout six months an' 'en I'd just' begin lettin' go little at time. I'd pull big, elegant hundehd out o' my cloze an' some one say, 'Boy, wheah you get 'at green stuff?' I say I win it on 'e faw'eign book. I'd p'ten' to be gamblin', un'e'stand? I'd go to New Yawk o' some othah place an' bring roll back an' tell 'em I win it."

"What are you givin' us? As soon as you got hold of that stuff you'd go down and buy all the blue clothes on Clark street."

"Then he'd get gay an' tell that Twenty-fourth Street girl all about it an' she'd tell somebody else an' they'd have him in the booby-hatch in about two hours."

At this there was general laughter, and the one who had been consigned to the "booby-hatch" laughed hoarsely after the others had quieted.

"No, seh; I guess I wouldn't betteh stay 'round' 'iss town," he said. "I get me one of 'em p'ivate Pullman cahs an' go traveling' 'roun' e' country. I wouldn' do thing — 'bout fo' cullud boys to wait on me. 'Heah, boy, open 'notheh box of e'm cigahs an' put two mo bottles on ice.' My goodness! Get into new town, wave my han' jus' like 'at — up come caih'age. Get in, you know, drive 'roun' mos' p'ominent thuhfaihs — "

"What's that last word.?"

"He do n't know. He heard somebody out on Armour Avenue say that."

"I'd be strong 'ith 'em cullud guhls too. My goodness, Miss Ruth, who's 'at new gemman 'ith all 'em di'mon's an' rubies. Yes, seh, I'd have 'em settin' traps faw me! Could n't keep 'em away nohow."

"I guess you've had some trouble already keepin' away that one you owe the laundry bill to."

"Hush! man!" and he laughed again. The barber at work had to poise his razor until he could control himself, while the man in the chair smiled through the lather.

"Le' me tell you — I'd pay 'at woman what I owe 'uh an' give huh hundehd dollah bill, an' 'en I'd neveh speak to huh agen. She eveh come up to me I say, 'Woman, I can't place you; go back to you' own kind o' people.'"

"A HOT MEMBEH"

"O, you'd get proud, would you? I do n't s'pose you'd speak to any of us, would you."

"I might 'membah seein' you somewheahs, but I sutny wouldn' know you ve'y well. I'd be too busy countin' money to fool my time on bahbehs. C'ose I'd let you have dollah o' two, but you wouldn' see me minglin' 'ith pooh men. You want to see me, you send in you' cahd by 'at cullud boy, an' I look it ovch an' say, 'Adams? Adams? Seems to me I see 'at name somewheahs. Tell 'im to wipe his feet an' come in.'"

"Yes, an' then you'd go in an' find him at a gold table, with a watermelon on one side of him and a fried chicken on the othcr."

"That ain' no bad guess, mistah! You can't tell, neetheh — might be po'teh-house steak 'ith onions. I'd jus' be settin' theah, stahvin' to death! You know I have all 'ese cullud men to wait on me — one to brush my close, one to shine my shoes, 'notheh to wait on 'e table, an' I'd have one cullud boy 'ith nothin' to do 'cept think o' what I want to eat. 'Heah boy, what you goin' o' gi' me f' suppeh?' 'Well,' he say, 'I got a little po'teh-house — an quail, an' pohk-chops — le's see, sweet potatoes, ice cream, chahlum-rushe —"

"Look out there!"

"O, got to have some of 'at stuff — cla'et, an' fancy cakes an' champagne."

"What are you talkin' about? You wuz n't built to stand anything better'n gin."

"See heah, misteh, when I'uze waitin' on e' table faw big banq'et an' gemman leave some of 'at champagne — I s'pose I took 'at wine an' th'owed it away, didn' I? Yes, seh, I used to get it befo' 'em little beads stop jumpin'."

Then there was a shuffle of feet, for some one had come down the stairway. A gruff voice asked, "Say, can you fix up these tans for me in a hurry?"

"Yes, seh, 'at's sutny jus' what I can do."

"While you 're rubbin' out that ten-cent piece you can think over some ways to spend that million."

" — When he gets it."

"The most money he ever had at one time was sixteen dollars.

That was when he got on that seven-to-one-shot. He did n't work for three days."

There was a sound of suppressed laughter in the corner. The man who had chanced into the place unfolded himself from the chair and saw the colored boy at work, throbbing with exertion.

"Brush!" shouted the barber, but the customer did not wait for the ceremonial. He ran for his car, and all the way home he leaned back in a warm reverie and helped the boy spend the million.

On Being Virtuous in Order to be Happy

Without confessing to himself that he remembered the first visit, he went to the shop one morning to have his shoes cleaned. The first conversation was the mere commonplace which passes between the employer and the employed. It related to the kind of polish to be used. Pink saw before him only a pair of shoes. He little suspected — but there is no need of anticipating.

The customer sat in an arm-chair which was placed on top of a box-like rostrum. The box and the chair were studded with brass tacks and other metal ornaments. They would have served as a Congo throne. William Pinckney Marsh usually had the market page of yesterday's paper tucked under the chair cushion.

Pink's shirt was a black and white study of trellises, with vines climbing up them.

The vest was double-breasted, and had been once polka-dot silk, but now the dots were mostly blurred away and the pockets had begun to ravel.

His trousers were black and brown check, worn thin at the knees and ragged at the bottom.

The shoes were extremely pointed, two sizes too large, cracked across the top and protuberant at the heel.

When Pink was dressed for the street he wore also a double-breasted coat tightly buttoned, a spreading blue necktie that had been handled once of twice too often, a high while collar and a light brown hat with a high crown. Pink improved as you studied him from the ground upward.

His apparel might have been judged as follows:

Shoes — Utterly disreputable.
Trousers — Shabby.
Coat — Badly worn.
Necktie — Showy.

Collar — Splendid.

Hat — Magnificent.

What need to tell of the coal-black face, the broad-flanged nose, the elastic mouth opening on teeth of pearly whiteness, and the close growth of kinky hair?

A song of passing popularity tells that all members of the Ethiopian division "look alike." Pink was one of a thousand — that is, so far as mere appearance was concerned.

When it came to a consideration of the higher being — the sure-enough ego — Pink was different. He saw things from his own standpoint, and there was room for no one else on his pedestal.

On this first morning he came to his task languidly, and even lazily. After some sleepy preparations, he drew a heavy sigh and attacked the shoes fiercely. It will never be known whether Pink was a tired mortal driven to work, or an industrious mortal who had to restrain himself by certain affectations.

He was at his best when he walked. He allowed his feet to shuffle so that the movement was a sort of slow dance-step.

He seemed to be keeping time to music which only the rapt and colored soul may hear.

The morning customer learned in two or three visits that the barbers liked Pink and pitied him. They were men who had given much study to public questions. Pink came in on their back-and-forth discussions. He pieced in observations which amused them, and also convinced them that Pink lacked seriousness of purpose. They regarded him as a sort of court jester. Sometimes they patronized him half in kindness, but they never forgot that there was a social chasm between a barber and a "brush."

Perhaps Pink did not fully understand the significance of their manner toward him, or he would have been cast down in spirit. As it was, the humility which he made his main stock in trade, was merely an outward pretense.

The morning customer learned this on the occasion of his third visit, up to which time the conversation had been along the lines of rather strict formality. At the second visit he crossed Pink's palm with silver, so that when he came the third time he saw a mellow smile in the corner. The barbers were talking on the relations of Church and State that morning.

THE MORNING CUSTOMER

The morning customer appeared to be amiable and receptive when Pink looked up at him.

"Listen at 'em toss 'at lang'age. Ain't they wahm? If you wan 'o know anything, you jus' come to 'em boys an' ask. If 'ey do n' know, no use to look in 'em books. It ain't theah — couldn' be."

"They 're up on everything, eh?"

"Oh-h-h, wise — wise boys. Cong'ess could n't tell 'em boys nothin' 'bout how to do it. No, seh, 'em rascals is sutny good."

Pink folded the drying-cloth and went at the shoe again, singing softly:

> "Misteh Johnson, tuhn me loose,
> Got no money but good es-cuse;
> O, Misteh Johnson, I wis't you would,
> Oh-h-h — "

"A new song?" asked the morning customer.

"Ain' it wahm?"

"Who's Mister Johnson?"

"Misteh Johnson, he's a coppeh. He come in on a small game o' craps, an' 'at's what 'at cullud fellow's singin' to him at 'e box."

"Does that song relate to one of your own experiences?"

"No, seh — me? I nevah got 'rested — faw rollin' craps — no, seh."

"What was it you got arrested for?"

"Who said I got 'rested?"

"O, you never were arrested, eh?"

Pink's elastic mouth widened, and he laughed so that he had to stop work.

"Look heah, man, who's been tellin' you 'bout me?"

"O, you have been arrested?"

"I got 'uh once, but it wuz n' no craps, no, seh."

"Chickens?"

"W'y, say, look heah, misteh, somebody been paintin' me bad to you. No, seh, 'ey done it to me faw what 'at judge called dis-ohdehly."

"How about it? Were you disorderly?"

"Them 'at could 'membeh what happened give in bad tes'imony. I had to dig up ol' six dollahs to keep out of 'at big black wagon. No, seh, I don' wan' no mo'."

"You'd been drinking, had n't you?"

"Yes, seh, 'at's what made me dange'ous — wuz 'at oil o' distuhb'ance. I don' wan' no mo' to do 'ith 'em coppehs an' blue wagons an' judges. Cullud man sutny can't beat 'at game."

"That's right," said the morning customer. 'Be virtuous, and you will be happy.'"

"What is 'at 'spression? Say it oveh, Be —"

"'Be virtuous, and you will be happy.'"

"O, I guess some one-ahm man wrote 'at! 'Be vuhchus, an' you will suahly be happy!' My goodness! I guess 'at's pooh lang'age! I sutny will use 'at on 'em Deahbohn Streets rascals. Yes, seh, I'll jus' brush you a few an' you sutny will be all right. Any time, Misteh, you goin' 'o th'ow 'at ovehcoat away, jus' th'ow it at me. No clothin' stoah eveh see 'at coat 'cept when you walk past. Ten — yes, seh — 'at's 'e propeh 'mount. Good day, seh. Misteh, have I got 'at? Be vuhchus, an' you will sutny be happy. Yes, seh — yo's truly — good day, seh."

On the Proper Observance of Christmas

The holiday season was at hand the next time the morning customer went to the shop. As he climbed into the chair he saw on the wall, within easy reach, a pasteboard box capped with a sprig of green. In the side of the box was a slit large enough to receive a silver dollar. Below it were the words: "Merry Xmas. Remeber the porter."

"What does that mean — 'Merry Xmas'?" asked the customer.

Pink shook his head slowly. "You know mighty well what 'at means, misteh. If I on'y had you' ej'cation I would n' be whippin' flannel oveh no man's shoes."

"I do n't see what education has to do with it. What is it, anyway — that 'Merry Xmas'?"

"Misteh Cliffo'd, on 'e secon' chaih, made it faw me. He says 'at's 'Me'y Ch'is'mas.'"

"That's a funny way to spell Christmas. What does the rest of it mean there — about remembering the porter?"

"My goodness, misteh, you ain' goin' 'o fo'ce me to come right out an' ask faw it, ah you?"

"Ask for what?"

Pink emitted a series of heaving sounds to indicate that he was amused.

"Mr. Clifford did a very fine job there," observed the customer.

"Who, Misteh Cliffo'd? He can do mos' anything. He's got watch-chain made out o' real haih, he made himself."

"He must be a versatile genius."

"I guess he — say, misteh, 'at wuz a wahm piece o' talk. What was 'at you say — he —"

"I say he must be a versatile genius."

"A vussitle gemyus — genimus."

"Genius — versatile genius."

"Vussitle gen'us — 'at's lolly-cooleh. If I on'y had a few like 'at I'd keep 'em ketchin' theah breaths, suah. What's 'e def'mition?"

"That means a man of varied accomplishments."

Pink worked a few minutes and allowed the definition to percolate. Then he observed with a sigh: "I could n' ketch 'em boys; not 'ith a laddeh. Too high."

The barber at chair No. 1 shouted "Brush!" and Pink shuffled away to attend to a thin man with a powdered complexion and gummy hair.

First he brushed the thin man, front and back, becoming more earnest in his efforts just as the man received a handful of small change. Pink held the overcoat, and after the thin man had worked into it, he reached under for the inside coat and pulled it down so violently that the thin man was bowed backward. While Pink was brushing the overcoat the thin man walked over and took his hat from the hook.

But he was not to escape so easily. Pink gently pulled the hat away from him and went in search of the small brush. He stood in front of the thin customer, and, holding the hat gingerly in the left hand, brushed it carefully, at the same time blowing off imaginary specks of dust.

While the thin man was waiting for his hat he casually put his right hand into the trousers pocket. Pink stopped brushing and scratched at an invisible spot or stain of some sort on the sleeve of the overcoat.

"Shine?" he inquired softly.

"Nope."

He continued to brush the hat.

The thin man withdrew his hand from the pocket. Pink turned the hat around right side forward and presented it to the customer with a bow. The customer's right hand moved forward a few inches, but Pink's broad palm met it more than half-way. The nickel passed.

"Thank you, seh," said Pink in a reverential whisper. The thin man started toward the door. Pink seized the long whisk-broom and pursued him, hitting him between the shoulder-blades. As the man passed out Pink got in one final blow on the coat-tails.

PART OF THE MORNING PAPER

"You're doing well to-day," observed the morning customer when Pink had returned to his place in the corner.

Pink dropped the nickel to the floor, as if by accident. Then he picked it up, turned it over and put it in his mouth.

"Money layin' all 'roun' heah to-day," he said, rattling the coin against his teeth.

"You can buy a loaf of bread with that," suggested the customer.

"You betteh make anothah guess on what I'm goin' 'o do 'ith any nicks I get hold of 'ese days. Bread's faw pooh people. I'm goin' 'o eat chidlin's, roas' pig, cawnpone, che'y pie, mash' tuhnips an' — le' me see — "

"You'll be lucky to get snowballs," interrupted the barber known as 'Misteh Adams,' who had strolled over to the corner to watch the boy at work.

"Don' lose no sleep 'bout me," retorted Pink. "I may be baihfoot an' need mo' undeh-cloze, but I sutny will have my childin's on Ch'is'mas, an' any man 'at thinks diff'ent wants to make a new guess, suah. If'at ol' box up on 'e wall uses me good I'll be a wahm baby 'iss Ch'is'mas — yes, seh, I'll eat oystehs 'ith my true love."

"How are you and that girl gettin' along now?" asked Mr. Adams, with a palpable wink at the morning customer.

"I do n' know nothin' 'bout no guhl," replied Pink with a sly grin. "No, seh, Misteh Adams, I got no money to waste on no piece o' calico. I'm jus' wantin' to feed myse'f 'iss Ch'is'mas. No use talkin'! You know what 'at col' wind say when it comes zoo-in an' whistlin' roun' 'e cohneh. It say, 'Boy, wheah's all 'at money you spent faw ice-cream an' neckties las' summch?'"

"Mistah Adams" walked away and Pink said, in a low tone: "You do n' ketch me tellin' any white bahbeh 'bout 'at lady."

"Have n't you got any money for Christmas?" asked the morning customer.

"No, seh, I got to get someping out of 'at box."

"You ought to be able to save a little money."

"Down theah wheah I live, misteh, it ain' safe f' man to have no money. If 'em tough cullud boys think you' savin' yo' coin 'ey jus' stop you at night an count it faw you. Yes, seh, an' when 'ey get th'ough countin' it, 'em boys han' back to you what 'ey do n' need. If anybody goin' o' spen' my money I want to spend it myse'f."

"Why do n't you put it in the bank?"

"Yes, seh, I'm goin' o' put some in 'e bank next yeah."

"Well, you want to bear well in mind that procrastination is the thief of time."

"Le' go, man! 'At's sutny 'e hottes' thing you handed me yet. Pocazzumalashum — prasticanashum — chenashalum — no, seh, thea h's one too good faw me. No, seh, don' try to gi' me 'at one. It keep me busy jus' foldin' kinks out of 'at boy."

"Why, that's very simple — procrastination. It means the habit of postponing action, putting off until to-morrow, as it were."

"'At's all right what 'at means, misteh. I ain' strong enough to swing 'at kind — pocrastumalation — timination —"

"Procrastination."

"No, seh, do n' try it, I can't use 'at boy. 'Ey would n' stan' faw nothin' like 'at on Deahbohn Street. You keep 'at one an' use it you'se'f — proclast-pocrasum-unn-unn — misteh, you sutny have wuhds up yo' sleeve 'at is strangehs to me."

"Procrastination is a good word," said the morning customer as he slipped a quarter into the Christmas-box and descended from the high-chair.

"Thank you, seh," repeated Pink, three times.

"'Ey's sutny ve'y few men can use 'em wuhds as you do," said he, as he was brushing the morning customer. "'Prastigumation is what steals away yo' time' — no, seh, do n' tell me no mo'; it's too high. Good mawnin'. Yes, seh. Same to you, misteh. Me'y Ch'is'mas."

On Winning the Affections of a Woman

The morning customer learned by experience that Pink thrived on a diet of long words. He could not determine whether Pink's admiration for these words was real or feigned, and it mattered little so long as the boy pretended to be in ecstasy.

One day, toward the close of the holiday season, the morning customer learned something of Pink's love affairs. This was really the beginning of his term as guide, counselor, and friend.

"Good morning, Pink," he said, as he came in. "I trust you have had your matutinal this morning."

"My goodness, misteh! I might have my pockets full of 'at stuff an' not know it. I ain't had nothin' 'iss mawnin' 'cept breakfas'."

"Got a morning paper?"

"I got paht o' one heah, misteh," and Pink reached under the chair for it.

"Part of one, eh? I suppose it's the page of small ads. You're the only man I ever knew who bought a newspaper on the installment plan. Why do n't you save up some morning and buy a whole paper — have a little enterprise about you? You want to get a new cushion in this chair too. Do n't you know you have to treat customers well in order to hold trade these days?"

Pink restrained his mirth and sighed with enjoyment.

"Misteh, you sutny good."

While he was working with the rough brush to remove the dry and encrusted mud, he sung softly:

> "I do n' love a-nobody,
> An' nobody loves me.
> Yo' afteh my money —
> Do n' caih faw me.
> I'm goin' o stay single,
> Always-a be free;
> I do n' love a-nobody,
> An' nobody loves me."

The morning customer folded the paper in his lap and listened to the song.

"Is that your private confession?" he asked.

"How's 'at, misteh?"

"You do n't love anybody, eh?"

"Co'se, misteh, I 'uz jus' singin' what it says in 'at song."

"O, I see. So you do love somebody, after all? I believe I've heard something about that girl out there."

"Out wheah, misteh — out wheah? You neveh saw 'at guhl in all yo' life, misteh. What you want to say 'at faw?"

"I did n't say I ever saw her. I said I'd heard about her."

Pink laughed to himself until his frizzled head bobbed up and down above the shoe. Then he looked up at the morning customer, his eyes big with doubt, and said, "Yo' stringin' me, misteh."

"Certainly not. I was talkin' to some colored boy the other day — I forget his name. I says to him: 'Do you know William Pinckney Marsh?' and he says: 'Do you mean Pink Marsh, the fellow that likes chicken so well?'"

"Who said 'at, misteh? Who was 'at cullud rascal 'at tried to make me out chicken-lifteh?"

"Do n't get excited. Keep right on with your work. He simply said that you liked chicken. He did n't say that you stole chickens."

"I know, misteh, but what is 'at he means by sayin' I like chicken? Do n't you know cullud man say someping like 'at 'bout anotheh an' he gen'ally got to lose a fight? Yes, seh, you say 'chickens' to cullud man, an' 'at means someping."

"Why, you *do* like chicken, do n't you?"

"How's 'at? W'y — misteh, even if I do, do n't all people like chicken?"

"I suppose they do, but this friend of yours says that you eat more chicken than any other colored fellow on the South Side."

"Who? Who? He say 'at, misteh? Goodness! Wis't you could 'membeh his name. I think I'd hahm 'at man if I get him placed. What else he tell you?"

"Well, he said you had a girl and that another fellow was trying to cut you out."

"Who — Gawge Lippincott?"

"Yes, that's the name, George Lippincott. This fellow seemed to think that George had a shade the best of it."

"Do n't you neveh believe it, misteh, not faw minute — no, seh. It ain't wrote in no book 'at Gawge Lippincott can do me at no game — no, seh."

"Who's the girl?"

"Young lady name Miss Lo'ena Jackson."

"Lorena, eh? That's a fancy name?"

"Yes, seh, an' little ol' Miss Lo'ena's hot membeh. She's so wahm you can feel 'e heat on otheh side of 'e street when she goes past. My goodness! I s'pose she's bad to look at. She had me settin' up nights faw 'while."

"Dark?"

"No, seh, not as dahk as me, but she ain' no blonde, neetheh. I s'pose 'at guhl ain' got no cloze. My goodness! Get on 'at puhl-cullud cloak 'ith all 'em buttons an' staht 'long Deahbohn Street — face at ev'y window, suah."

"Does she reciprocate your affection?"

"Do n' make me jump faw 'em, mistah. What is 'at — 'cip'ocate?"

"Does she love you?"

"Misteh, I'm real thing jus' now, but I can't p'omise no finish. I'm playin' hahd, but if 'at lady eveh calls me —" and Pink once more shook with laughter.

"I do n't understand you."

"I tell you, misteh. When I staht in to win 'at lady Gawge Lippincott 'uz ve'y strong theah. She couldn' see me. Gawge got me beat on ej'cation. We be oveh Mis' Willahd's house — ol' Gawge on sofy — 'Miss Lo'ena, I'm afraid 'e weatheh goin' 'o be mo' 'centrical on 'count of 'at atmosphe'cal management,' someping like 'at. She come back jus' as wahm as he wuz. Me, misteh? Jus' settin' theah an' bein' counted out. I wuz n't in 'at cullud society no mo'n if I'd been white. When it come to tossin' lang'age ol' Gawge sutny had me skinned. Jus' same, I figgah out what I got to do to get nex' to 'at lady. I know Miss Lo'ena wants wheel —'cuz Jennie Tayloh's got one in 'e same house, an' kin' o' been th'owin' it into Lo'ena 'bout not bein' in line. One night I 'uz talkin' to Lo'ena an' I say, 'What kin' of a wheel is 'at Jennie Tayloh's got?' an' she say, 'I think,

Misteh Mahsh, it's one 'at huh motheh bought at secon'-han' stoah.'
Knockin',' un'estand? I say, 'Miss Lo'ena, what kin' o' wheel you like
bes',' an' she says she like 'at Genemvieve wheel. I pull out my little
book an' write someping in it. I ask huh what size, an' she say,
'Twent'-six,' an' I say 'Twent'-six,' an' into 'e book, un'estan', mistch?
'Black saddle o' tan saddle?' an' she say 'Tan.' Down it goes into 'at
book. You jus' ought to see 'em eyes. 'Misteh Mahsh, what you
puttin' into 'at book?' 'Neveh you min'. You find out some day.' My
goodness, misteh! I own 'at lady f'om 'at minute. She know mighty
well why I put all 'at in 'e book. Nex' day she goes an' tells Jennie
Tayloh, 'Misteh Mahsh goin' o' buy me Genemvieve wheel.' I
s'pose she's usin' me bad now."

"Well, are you going to get the wheel?"

"W'y, misteh, you ought to know me betteh 'n 'at. Way things is
comin' now I could n' buy 'at chain 'at goes on 'e back wheel. I
could n' buy 'nough keh'sene to fill 'at little lamp 'at hangs on in
front. Lo'ena knows I'm goin' 'o buy huh wheel jus' 'e same. Walkin' 'long otheh evenin' an' I say, 'Miss Lo'ena, when's yo' buhth-
day,' and tell me, 'Tenth o' Mahch, but what you want know 'at
faw?' an' I say, 'O, 'at 's all right, neveh mind!' Look heah, man,
when it come tenth o' Mahch and no wagon backs up theah 'ith a
wheel in it — you know! I'll be cold wheat-cake, an' no mistake!
She'll have Gawge Lippincott back on huh staff, suah 'nough."

"Well, do you think it's right to trifle with a young lady's affections in that manner?"

"Do n't you botheh 'bout 'at lady, misteh. She ain' nobody's fool.
She eveh get a wheel out o' me she'd th'ow me in 'e aih an' staht
out to fin' some suckeh to buy one of 'em bloomeh suits faw huh.
Yes, seh, she's full of 'at ol' con. She think she got me right now. I
tol' huh 'e otheh evenin', 'Lo'ena, I'd like to go an' have some
oystehs 'iss ev'nin', but 'e fact is I'm savin' ev'y cent o' money I can
get hold of.' Well, co'se she knows what I'm savin' faw — got to
have 'at wheel by Mahch, no use talkin'. O, I do n't know! I s'pose
I'm foolish! I neveh seen cullud lady till I met Miss Lo'ena."

"What do you think will happen when this girl finds out for certain that you're not going to give her a bicycle?"

"Neveh you mind. I'll fix 'at all right. I'll get mad at huh an' give 'at wheel to somebody else. I'll give it to cullud lady on 'e Nawth Side."

"O, I see. Well, Pink, I did n't think you'd be guilty of such malfeasance."

"She'd do me jus' as much 'feasance if she got chance. She's out afteh 'at new wheel, an' 'at's why I'm ol' papa in 'e pahloh now. Befo' I sprung 'at wheel game, Gawge Lippincott had me done easy — had me faded. I kind o' like 'at lady, but she can't neveh get me foolish enough to let go o' no coin; no, seh."

"How much does a wheel cost?"

"Goodness, misteh, keep still! What's 'e use? I s'pose 'at wheel I'm goin' o' buy faw Lo'ena cost eighty dollahs. Hush, man! If I on'y had 'at much I would n' be foolin' 'ith Miss Lo'ena Jackson. I'd be wahm boy 'ith 'em swell cullud people down towahds Thuhtieth Street — yes, seh, you could n' lose me."

"Well, that's all right. If you rub those shoes much longer you'll wear them out. Here is your piece of silver. I have enjoyed very much the story of your amour."

"Deahbohn — not Ahmoh," said Pink.

The morning customer laughed aloud, and Pink laughed sympathetically, without knowing why he did so. He brushed the morning customer out to the stairway.

On War With England

The morning customer was permitted to see the photograph of Miss Lorena Jackson. He looked at it with evident interest and said, "Stylish, is n't she?"

"Who? 'At guhl? High-steppeh. She's got 'em cloze, an' she knows how to weah 'em.

He put the photograph back into a hidden coat pocket and laughed secretively.

The morning customer waited a few minutes and then asked. "How is everything around the place — quiet?"

"Yes, seh, it's ve'y quiet 'iss mawnin'. Betteh le' me put in new paih o' laces faw you, misteh. On'y ten cents, seh."

"Well, you go ahead and shine those shoes and we'll talk about the laces later on."

"Yes, seh, sutny, on'y these heah laces is fah gone."

"Pink, are you criticising my personal appearance?"

"No, seh, I do n' mean no c'iticizin', on'y if you wan' paih o' laces I know wheah you can get 'em."

"Never mind the laces now. I do n't come here to discuss sordid commercial transactions. Let us lift our conversation into the higher realms. Let's talk about art, or something like that."

"My goodness, misteh, when it comes to me holdin' up my end o' talk 'ith you I'm no betteh 'n one-legged man at a cake-walk," and he gurgled.

"How are you and Mr. Clifford getting along?"

"Did n' you heah 'bout it? Did n' you heah what happen' heah yes'day? Misteh Cliffo'd done it all, too. He 'uz 'e gen'al an' e' whole ahmy — yes, seh."

"What was it?"

"We had wah 'ith Englan' heah yes'day — O, bad, too. Ouah side win, though. Gen'al Cliffo'd made wahm fight."

"MISTEH CLIFFO'D"

"How did it start?"

"I do n' know. Gen'al Cliffo'd 'uz settin' oveh theah by 'e table, an' 'fo I know 'bout it he had ahmy o' fo' million soljahs an' 'uz mahchin' right oveh to do Englan'."

"How did he get them across the ocean?"

"I do n' know, seh. I s'pose he made 'em swim. He had 'em all oveh theah chasin' 'at English ahmy 'fo' I un'e'stood what it 'uz all 'bout. Gen'al Cliffo'd 'uz full o' trouble. He put up betteh fight 'n Gen'al Grant eveh did. Co'se Misteh Adams, on 'e thuhd chaih, he'ped some. Misteh Adams 'uz gen'al of all 'e ships. I guess it did n' take him mo' 'n ten minutes to sink all of 'em otheh ships. Goodness, mistah, I neveh see such wah in a bahbeh-shop befo' in all my life."

"What had England been doing?"

"How's 'at? Man, what could ol' Englan' do 'ith Gen'al Cliffo'd an' 'ese fo' million soljahs up an' a' comin'?"

"I know, but why did Mr. Clifford make war on England?"

"It 'uz someping 'bout Venzalum — Venazulum."

"O, Venezuela! Why, that's all settled. Great Britain has agreed to our terms, and the whole difficulty is to be submitted to arbitration."

"Yes, seh, I un'e'stand. Misteh Adams 'uz speakin' to gemman in his chaih 'bout 'iss 'batation 'at Misteh Cliffo'd read 'bout in 'e mawnin' papeh. Misteh Adams tell 'iss gemman 'at 'e reason Englan' lay down is 'at Uni'd States could do 'uh up if it eveh come to case o' scrap. 'En 'iss gemman in Misteh Adams's chaih he says 'at Englan' got mo' ships 'an us an' mo' soljahs, 'an' might do 'iss country if it come to show-down. 'En Misteh Cliffo'd gets out his fo' million soljahs an' begins. Goodness, misteh! We jus' had wah faw 'n houah. One minute, you know, Misteh Cliffo'd oveh theah by 'e table he'd be killin' 'bout hund'ehd thousan' men and 'en Misteh Adams at 'e thuhd chaih he put some of 'ese 'pedoes — "

"Torpedoes."

"Yes, seh, t'pedoes — he'd put some o' 'em undeh Englan' ship an' blow 'uh all to pieces. Misteh Cliffo'd, he say: 'W'y, do n' talk to me' bout Englan'. We done huh fo' times an' we can do it agen. I neveh see a man so wahm faw trouble. All 'iss time Misteh Adams blowin' up ships."

"England had no chance at all?"

"Misteh, no mo' chance 'an a sheep 'ith a butcheh. You know Gen'al Cliffo'd had eight million men 'fo' he got th'ough. Yes, seh, I think he got two hund'ehd thousan' heah in 'iss town. I tell you, we couldn' lose 'e way Gen'al Cliffo'd had it fixed yes'day. 'Fo' he got th'ough he had all 'at Englan' belongin' to 'iss country. You know 'at big town in Englan'?"

"London?"

"Yes, seh, 'at 's it. How long you s'pose it took Gen'al Cliffo'd an' his ahmy to mahch right in an' capchah 'at town?"

"I have n't the slightest idea."

"Two days, seh. Gen'al Cliffo'd an' his ahmy got oveh theah one day an' 'ey wuzn' feelin' ve'y well, so 'ey kind o' hang 'round 'e fuhst day loadin' up 'em guns an' washin' 'e buggies an' 'en nex' mawnin' 'ey go on oveh to London. I think 'ey got theah 'bout ten o'clock in 'e mawnin'. 'Iss heah gen'al at London he come out an' size up Gen'al Cliffo'd an' 'ese fo' million white bahbehs, an' tries to put up fight, but, my goodness, man, 'at gen'al ought to see his finish 'e minute he go 'genst Gen'al Cliffo'd. It couldn' come out on'y one way. A little while an' 'em Englishmen gettin' out of 'e way jus' like cullud boys goin' out o' Johnson's back dooh afteh razah play — same thing. Gen'al Cliffo'd got on white hoss, misteh, and rode into 'at town 'ith band playin' 'at 'Wash'nin Pos' Mahch.' Yes, seh, 'at secon' day he sutny showed up ve'y strong. He made Gen'al Grant look like lame man."

"In the meanwhile, I suppose Mr. Adams was destroying the English navy — the English ships."

"O, easy, easy, easy! 'Iss same aftehnoon 'at Misteh Cliffo'd — I mean Gen'al Cliffo'd — 'uz ridin' 'e white hoss an' smokin' fifteen-cent cigah, Misteh Adams done up 'e las' English ship — yes, seh, he done up ev'ything. 'Iss gemman in Misteh Adams's chaih he wants to know what Misteh Adams goin' 'o do when 'em English ships come up close to 'at New Yawk City an' staht tossin' wahm cannon balls oveh on 'e houses."

"I suppose Mr. Adams had that all provided for."

"You know it! Yes, seh, 'at wuz an easy one. Misteh Adams got kind o' i'on raft 'at jus' stuck up oveh 'e wateh 'bout foot, an' he took 'iss out to 'at place wheah all 'em otheh ships had to come past, an' 'en ev'y time ship come 'long he'd th'ow ol' dym'nite bum oveh an' blow it up. I guess he blowed up 'bout ten ships in one day. No use tryin', misteh, you can't lose 'at Misteh Adams at no game eveh played. If Englan' eveh fin's out what Misteh Adams got up his sleeve, she won't eveh have no trouble 'ith us, no, seh."

"Well, I am glad to learn that we can whip England."

"W'y, misteh, I tell you we done it already — right heah in 'iss shop yes'day."

"What part did you take in the fratricidal strife?"

"Change it, misteh! Come down!"

"Were you in the fight?"

"No, seh, I set back heah by 'e stove dodgin' bullets. I neveh see such wah. 'Fo' it 'uz oveh I kind o' felt soh'y faw 'em English people. Did n' have thing left when Gen'al Cliffo'd got th'ough. Me an' 'at new bahbeh is 'e on'y ones 'at wuzn' in 'e wah."

"That's so. You have a new barber, have n't you?"

"Yes, seh, I'm kind o' 'fraid o' him, too. You see 'at white tie he weahs. Look out faw 'em, misteh. 'Ey's eitheh ve'y good o' ve'y bad 'at weahs 'em white ties. We had bahbeh heah 'at wo' tie like 'at one, an' one night 'e got all 'e razahs in his pockets an' moved. Yes, seh, he changed his scenery. He 'uz a quiet boy, too, 'ith one of 'em Zion Meth'dis' neckties."

"Are you through? Well, I tell you what I want, if you have any, and that's a pair of new shoe-laces."

"My goodness, misteh!"

On the Efficacy of Dreams

The next time the morning customer came in he found Pink locked in an earnest debate with Mr. Clifford. The barber was "honing" a razor and debating with careless ease, as one who knew and scorned the full resources of his opponent. Pink had an ominous forefinger in the air and was contending for something or other in relation to civil rights.

"No, seh! no, seh, I do n' mean 'at, Misteh Cliffo'd," he said. "I do n' mean to 'sinuate 'at a cullud man ought to do anything 'at a white pusson does, but what ahgament I make, Misteh Cliffo'd, is 'at he's got right to do it undeh ouah law. Did n' Misteh Ab'ham Lincoln settle all 'at business? I guess he sutny did. Ab'ham said a few things 'at set 'em guessin'."

"Why, the only mistake we ever made was in settin' you folks free," said Mr. Clifford, with a wink at the barber at the next chair.

Pink laughed aloud, and then said: "O, no, seh, Misteh Cliffo'd, you do n' mean 'at."

"Course I do. You ain't no good when you work for yourself. There's a man been waitin' in your chair for five minutes while you was talkin' to me."

Pink hurried over to the morning customer with many expressions of apology.

"My, goodness, misteh, I did n' see you. I'm ve'y soh'y, seh. If 'ey's one thing I prides myself 'bout, seh, it's bein' right heah, seh, on deck ready faw business at all houahs. 'At's 'e on'y way to get yo' good customehs an' keep 'em comin' to you, yes, seh. I can't get too many comin' my way, suah as yo' bawn."

"What was all this discussion about?"

"'At's all right, misteh; do n't you feel bad about it an' I won't. Misteh Cliffo'd got it settled 'ith himse'f 'at he's ve'y wahm pusson. No, seh, you could n' make him b'lieve nothin' else. W'y, misteh, he sets heah ev'y day an' tells 'ese oteh wise boys 'bout what 'at mayah oveh in 'e City Hall ought to do. If 'at theah mayah'd on'y come oveh heah ev'y mawnin' an find out f'om Misteh Cliffo'd how things stood, he sutny could n' make no mistakes. 'Spose Misteh Cliffo'd picks up papeh wheah it tells 'bout a killin'. Well, seh, he reads it oveh, spellin' out 'em long oncs — he ain' such a hot readeh — an' when he's th'ough he tuhns to Misteh Adams an' he say, 'I know who done 'at muhdeh. It wuz 'at woman 'at find 'e revolveh.' He knows in a minute. You can't fool 'at boy."

"I think he ought to be chief of police," said the morning customer.

Pink stopped work and shook with suppressed laughter.

"Yo' sutny all right, mistch," said he, "You know, misteh, I can't une'stan' why all 'ese waluu boys 'at knows mo' an' any one else 'at eveh come oveh 'e bridge is all down heah in 'is ol' shop, crawlin' heads faw tow bits, when 'ey ought to be up in one of 'em sky-scrapehs — you know, misteh — big desk, an' you push one of 'em bells an' say: 'Boy, take 'bout thousan' dollahs out of 'e safe an' put it in my ovehcoat pocket; I'm goin' out to meet a few frien's.' 'At's wheah all 'ese boys'd be if 'ey wuz half as waluu as 'ey say they ah."

"You do n't seem to have a very high opinion of your tonsorial associates."

"Listen at you toss 'em wuhds!" said Pink, glancing up in rapture. "Oteh foot, misteh. O, well, seh, 'bout white bahbehs — it do n' pay to have no trouble 'ith 'em. Jus' let 'em think 'ey's 'e real thing, an' you on'y pooh cullud boy, tryin' to do 'e best he can, an' yo' all right. Call 'em misteh so-and-so. 'At's someping 'ey do n't of'en get an' it jollies 'em. Bu' le' me tell you someping, misteh. I'll be eatin' bread 'ith gravy on it when some of 'ese white bahbehs makin' mahks in 'e snow."

"By the way, how is your bank account coming on? You told me, did n't you, that you were going to begin to save money after the first of the year?"

Pink leaned over the shoe and brushed with great energy, but said nothing. The customer heard sounds similar to those made by a loose steam-valve, and upon looking down he saw that Pink was smothering with laughter, which he was trying to hold in. This kind of mirth is contagious. The morning customer began to laugh.

"Misteh, yo' sutny all right," said Pink, without looking up.

"How much have you saved?"

"Misteh, all 'ese heah banks can bust an' 'ey wont eveh touch me."

"I thought you were saving up."

"Yes, seh; 'at 's right."

"You've been saving up, but you have n't got anything yet — is that it?"

"Misteh, if I got it all togetheh I'd jus' 'bout have pohk chops an' no mo'."

"What have you been doing with your money?"

"In 'e fus' place, misteh, I do n' take in as much as Misteh Mahshall Field o' Misteh P. D. Ahmoh."

"I see. You've been playing policy again."

"Jus' once in while, seh."

"Have any luck?"

"Yes, seh; I come 'ithin one numbeh o' gettin' sisteen dollahs. One ev'nin' at Mis' Willa'd's house we had aigs faw suppeh, fried in fat an' potatoes sliced in. I eat about six o' seven aigs, an' en' all night dream aigs. I go pas' stoahs an' I see hund'ehds o' baskets full o' aigs, an' I think I'm eatin' fried aigs all 'e time? so nex' mawnin' I suhch myself an' fin' twenty cents an' put it on 'e ol' aigs row."

"Why did n't you play it on the indigestion row?"

"In'geschun?" asked Pink, wonderingly.

"Go on with your story. What was the egg row?"

"Yes, seh; aig row 'uz fo'-fo'teen-fawty. Fo' come, misteh, an' ol' fawty, but fo'teen used me mean."

"How much did you win?"

"Do n't you un'e'stand 'at game, misteh? You got to ketch all three. If 'at ol' fo'teen'd used me right — say, I'd be spohtin' oveh-coat 'ith fo' rows o' buttons."

"But fourteen did n't come out, did it?"

"No, seh. 'At dream 'uz all right, on'y fo'teen would n't come out."

"I do n't see what good it did you to have two numbers come, as long as you did n't win."

"It sutny showed 'ey wuz someping in 'at dream."

"All right. I am glad you can see it in that light. Where do you play policy, anyway? I thought all those places were closed up."

"Misteh, I neveh see time yet when I could n' bet my b'lief, no,

seh. You got to weah rubbehs some times to get at 'e man 'ith 'e
sheet, but I neveh kep' no money I wanted to lose, not yet, seh."

"Well, that's a funny thing. I've lived in this town for ten years,
and I never saw a policy-shop yet. I do n't know what one of them
would look like."

"Yo' cullah's wrong, misteh; yo' cullah's sutny wrong. White pusson can't find 'em games, no matteh how long he hunts, but cullud
boy — put blin'fold on him, tuhn him loose in 'at alley, an' he jus'
feel his way to some place wheah man's puttin' numbehs on 'e
sheet. Culled boy can smell row o' numbehs faw two blocks. Yes,
seh; 'at's no fab'cashun, neetheh."

"Fabrication? That's a good word."

"'At's a ve'y sassy wuhd, misteh. Misteh 'Stein, 'e cigah-man,
han' me 'at one yes'day. 'At means yo' lyin', do n' it?"

"Yes, a fabrication is anomalous to a lie. It is frequently used as
a synonym, although if I were to cogitate with exactitude I would
say that it refers rather to a fanciful invention. Of course, you understand, Pink, that there are many terms allied in paraphristic
connection which are essentially — ah — dissimilar when it comes
right down to it. Have you got change for a quarter? Thanks. Well,
I must meander toward my destination. That's a good shine you
gave me. I hope you will not become egotistical by reason of my
eulogiums. By George! It's nearly nine o'clock."

The morning customer hurried toward the door, leaving Pink
open-mouthed and staring into vacancy. He was in a waking
dream, and the broom swung in his limp hand. His lips moved, but
no sound came forth.

On the Powers of the Chief Executive

From the day on which the morning customer defined the word "fabrication" he became the court of last resort. On the occasion of his first succeeding visit he was called on to settle a dispute.

"Misteh, I want you to tell me someping, 'cuz I know you can tell it to me right," began Pink.

"I do n't know that I can. You must n't ask me anything hard."

"'At's all right, seh. If I had yo' ej'cation I would n't be scaihed o' no question in 'e book. If I on'y had as many fac's in my head as you got I'd win mo'n one bet f'om some of 'em wise Af'o-Ameh'-cans out theah on Deahbohn Street."

"You've got Afro-Americans out there, have you?"

"Yes, seh; I neveh know I 'uz one of 'em till 'bout two weeks ago. Ain't safe to call cullud man coon no mo' any mo' 'an it is to say 'niggeh.' My goodness, misteh! Do n' like to be called dahkies neetheh. It use to be Eth'op'ans, but now it's Af'o-Ameh'cans. 'At 's a ve'y wahm name. Since 'ey begin to use 'at name I would n' change my cullah faw no money."

"What is the dispute you were asking about?"

"Yes, seh. I tell you. It 'uz a 'spute I had 'tween me an' Willis Tuckeh at Miss Willa'd's house last ev'nin'. Willis begin by askin' me who I'd ratheh be, Misteh Presiden' McKinley o' Misteh Potteh Palmeh. I say I ratheh be Misteh McKinley, faw even if I did n' have as much money I could give p'sitions to all my frien's an' get good livin' faw nothin'. Willis want to know how I figgah it, an' I say 'at 'e Presiden of 'iss heah land can say to any man he likes, 'Heah, you go to Eu'ope faw me an' spend all 'e money you need an' have good time.' 'Notheh thing, too, I say, Misteh McKinley he get anything he wants f'om 'e gov'ment. If he want new fuhnichah in 'e house wheah he lives he jus' send out an' get it an' have 'e bill sent to Cong'ess. It don' cost him a cent. He sutny have a snap, I say. Now, misteh, I want to know am I right what I say 'bout 'e Presiden'.'"

"Well, what did Willis say?"

"Yes, seh, Willis claim to me Misteh McKinley could n' buy nothin' 'ceptin' Cong'ess say it 'uz all right. I tell him, 'Man yo' foolish; 'at Presiden' comes puht neah bein' 'e whole thing bout 'iss gov'ment.' You le' me be Presiden' faw twenty minutes some time an' I would n' neveh shine no mo' shoes f' no man.''

"That's right. I suppose you'd order everything in sight, and have it charged up to Congress."

"Hush, man! I would n' do thing! 'At's what I tell Willis. I say Misteh Presiden' McKinley can buy anything he wants an' Cong'ess got to pay faw it. Willis say Presiden' got to ask Cong'ess 'bout it befo'-hand an' 'en if 'ey say it's all right, he goes 'head an buys it.''

"I do n't think Willis knows very much about the functions of the Executive."

"Fum-shun? Say, misteh, if I could say 'at jus' e' way you done it I would n' let Willis Tuckeh o' no otheh man sew me up in no ahgament, no seh. What's 'at you mean by 'at 'bout fum shun?''

"I mean that your friend Willis is mistaken. That would be a fine state of affairs, would n't it — the President of the United States going around to Congress to get a little money every time he wants to buy some groceries?"

"Misteh, you know I use 'most 'em ve'y wuhds to Willis Tuckeh? I claim, seh, 'at no man has mo' to say 'bout 'e gov'ment 'an Misteh Presiden' McKinley. Am I true in 'at?''

"Certainly you are. You tell your friend to go and read the constitution of the United States."

"Who — Willis Tuckeh? No, seh; he ain' no friend o' mine. I'm jus' ready heah an' now to buy ticket to his fune'al. Yes, seh — he done me duht."

"You appear to cherish an animosity toward Mr. Tucker."

"I got 'mosity faw any man 'at hol's out on you. Yes, seh, what 'at speckled houn' done to me I ain' goin' 'o fawget ve'y soon."

"What's your grievance?"

"I do n' say I grieve 'bout it. When he say to me, 'No, seh, Pink, I did n' get it on,' I jus' say, 'O!' — like 'at — an' p'ten' like to believe

him, but I know con when I get it. 'Ey can make me take it, misteh,
but no man can't make me like it — no, seh!"

"What was it he was supposed to 'get on'?"

"I tell you, seh. 'Bout fo' weeks ago, I dream nothin' but flowehs.
I seem walkin' in fields 'ith nothin' but jus' flowchs as fah as I could
see. I'd see sunflowehs and mawnin'-glo'ies an' pinks an' ev'y kind
o' flowehs — mo'n I eveh seen befo' in all my life. Well, seh, nex'
mawnin' I kep' thinkin' 'bout 'em flowehs, an' I say, ''At sutny
means someping.' Afteh breakfas' I stops in at Clem Lesteh's
bahbeh-shop on State Street an' see in his book 'at if you dream
wil' flowehs, 'e row is three — seven — twenty-eight, an' if it's
flowehs done up in bo'quets, you want to play nine — thuhty —
fift'-two. Well, seh, I seen all kind o' flowehs, so I jus' say I play wil'
flowahs an' bo'quets, both."

"What is this play — policy again?"

"Yes, seh, two rows, jus' as I say, one faw wil' flowehs an' one
faw bo'quets. I 'uz jus' goin' out of 'e shop an' I meet Willis Tuckeh.
I say, 'Willis, I got to huh'y down to 'e shop an' I want you to take
quahteh an' split it on two sets o' numbehs I got heah. I had 'em
wrote down, misteh, an' I give 'em to him. I play nick in Frankfo't
book f' three — seven — twenty-eight and straddle ten 'tween
Frankfo't an' Kentucky on same row and let 'e otheh dime go on
straddle f' nine — thuhty — fift'-two. Willis p'omised me he'd see
'at 'e money got on faw aftehnoon drawin'.'"

"And then he did n't do it, eh?"

"Yes, seh, he done it, an' 'at's what makes me soah. W'y, misteh,
when I get th'ough my wuhk 'at day an' go to Misteh Lesteh's shop
and see ol' nine an' ol' thuhty an' ol' fift-two all in 'e row on 'e sheet,
I could jus' see myse'f countin' money. My goodness, misteh, I ask
faw Willis, an' no one seen him. I go oveh to his house. 'No,' Mis'
Tuckeh say, 'I ain't seen Willis since mawnin'. So I stahts 'long 'e
line. I want to save some of 'at eight. Last I fin' Willis in 'Lias
Clahk's saloon rubbin' 'genst 'e bah an' two crap-playehs along. Jus'
soon's I see 'at boy, misteh, I knowed it wuzn' no wateh made 'em
eyes 'at cullah. Cullud man can't get red in 'e face, but his eyes get
bad, an' ol' Willis he had Tom gin eyes when I find him. I say, 'Willis, will you give 'em to me in papch o' silveh?' He act su'prise like

an' say, 'What you talkin' 'bout?' I say, ''At secon' row win in 'e Frankfo't book.' Well, seh, when I said 'bout winnin', he made 'e wahmes' bluff I eveh see. O, he's good, Willis is. He says, 'By Gawge, Pink, I clean fawgot to get 'em numbehs,' an' 'en he han' me back 'at nasty ol' quahteh. I made no holleh, misteh. I neveh let on, but did n' I know 'at man had my rightful money right in his cloze? I went 'roun' to 'e policy-shop to look at 'e betsheet, but ol' Willis 'uz too keen faw me. He'd gone an' bet it somewheahs else. Yes, seh, he done me up. My goodness, misteh, I get so mad ev'y time I re'lize 'bout lettin' him do me. He done me right, suah. Un'e'stand, if numbehs didn't come, ol' Willis say to me, 'Heah's 'e tickets, Pink,' an' 'en he hand you some dead numbehs. If 'e row *did* come, he cash in an' keep all 'e velvet an' gi' me back my coin. Misteh, I jus' figgah I did n' have no show faw my life 'ith 'at man.''

"I suppose not. I'm surprised, however, that any of your Afro-American acquaintances would be guilty of such duplicity."

"'Plicity, misteh? I wan' tell you, Willis Tuckeh's wuhse 'an 'at. He's chicken-lifteh. When he goes 'long an alley, chickens come out an' roost on him. I know all 'bout his cha'ctch now. He can't neveh place no mo' money faw me. No, seh!"

On the Origin of Species

After a brief experience as oracle to Pink, the morning customer decided to be infallible. He learned that Pink came to him with full trust, and he believed it the better plan to answer all questions. So he found it his task to settle the problems relating to life and the after-life. Such a task would have been difficult but for the fact that Pink hung upon his words in simple faith and was not disposed to cross-question. One morning the subject matter was evolution.

"Misteh, I'm goin 'o ask you someping 'at me an' Misteh Cliffo'd 'uz 'sputin' 'bout 'iss mawnin'," said Pink pouring some of the soft dressing into the clay-colored bowl of his hand. "Misteh Cliffo'd says 'at 'iss heah Bob Inge'soll claim 'at all cullud people use to be suah' nough monks, same as 'ey got out heah at Lincum Pahk."

"The theory of evolution is that all men came from the lower orders of animal life," said the morning customer. "If Mr. Clifford says that the colored people in particular are descendants of the simian, he is laboring under a misapprehension."

"I tol' Misteh Cliff'od he 'uz givin' me mis'plehension, 'cuz you know, I may be easy, but 'ey can't shoot nothin' like 'at into me, no, seh."

"Does Mr. Clifford believe in evolution?"

"Mistah, what is 'at emvalution?"

"I believe it is defined as a change, by continuous differentiation and integration, from a simple homogeneity to a complex heterogeneity, or something like that."

"All right, misteh, heah's wheah I get off. 'Iss is my cohneh. Goodness, man! You ah sutny holdin' back mo' good talk an' any pusson I eveh see. 'Ferenchiashum of 'genity — I guess 'at's pooh talk, ain't it? I'm glad you handed 'at to me. I been kind o' wantin' to get 'at cleahed up in my mind. I know it now, misteh. Need n' say it agen."

The morning customer lifted the newspaper to conceal his grin of self-satisfaction, and Pink labored at the shoe, occasionally shaking his head and whispering to himself.

Finally he looked up and said, "I tol' Misteh Cliffo'd I could n't un'c'stand 'at, 'cuz I know 'at ol' Adam was 'e fus' man of all. Ain't 'at so?"

"That's right. We all descended from Adam."

"Yes, seh, an' Misteh Cliffo'd ask me how it is 'at we got white people an' cullud people. He kind o' had me guessin'. How 'bout 'at, misteh?"

"Why, that's easy enough. We were all white once, but some of the people went down into Africa just after the flood, and it was so hot down there that they became tanned."

"You call 'at tan?" asked Pink, thoughtfully looking at his knuckles, which resembled a row of chocolate creams. "No, seh, misteh, 'at ain't no tan. You sutny got to skin me to change my cullah. No, seh. Huh-uh! S'pose I go in Audito'um hotel to get dinneh 'an 'e whole thing 'ith one of 'em Gawgy minstrels suits come up an' say, 'Niggeh, you get out 'o heah befo' we take you out piece at a time!' I say, 'S'cuse me, seh, I'm no niggeh; I'm white man 'at go sunbuhned!' Co'se 'at 'd be all right! He'd un'c'stand 'at! Any man look at me know 'ey's nothin' 'e matter 'cept I'm kind o' flushed f'om bein' outdoohs."

"Well, I do n't deny that the color is fixed now, but you must remember that it required many generations for the African to assume his present color."

"Yes, seh, it's goin' 'o be two o' three yeahs 'fo' I change back to be blonde too," said Pink, and he gave an explosive bark of laughter.

"What's the matter with you, over there?" asked the new barber, with the white tie, who was sea-foaming a red-headed man and getting some good color-effects.

"Neveh you mind," returned Pink, 'I'm findin' out things. Look heah, misteh, how is it some cullud people's so dahk an' othehs jus' yellow? I s'pose some of 'em set in 'e shade mo' 'an othehs."

"I do n't know, I'm sure," said the morning customer, trying to restrain a smile.

"I guess 'at what you say 'bout changin' cullah ain't so fah off, neetheh. I use' to know cullud boy in Tuhkish bath place 'at got job on 'e stage doin' buck-dancin', an' some of 'at pasamala wahm stuff. He could jus' melt 'e nails out of 'e flooh, Albe't could. Ev'ybody thought Albe't 'uz a cullud boy till 'e got 'iss job 'ith 'e show. W'y, he wuzn' no coon at all, no, seh."

"What was he?"

"Yes, seh; he was a creole, 'at 's what Albe't wuz. Co'se you look at Albe't an' you might think 'at he had some niggeh blood in him, but he ain't. No, seh, he's a creole. I know it, 'cuz I see it on 'e show-bills. Good many people 'at used to be cullud is tuhnin' out to be creoles, oct'oons, Eth'op'ans, Af'o-Ameh'cans, an' —

"Any Cubans?"

"Yes, seh, some — smoked Cubans. Goodness, misteh, you can't hahdly find no mo' coons on 'e South Side. I think I betteh be creole myse'f, same as Albe't."

"How are you on dancing, Pink?"

"Wahm — wahm, an' no mistake. You neveh see me pick 'em up an' set 'em down agen, did you? I fool you, misteh; I ain't so bad. No, seh! But I sutny got to hang my head when ol' Albe't begin movin' 'round in 'e sand. Albe't got me faded, suah. Albe't went up to rent-rag 'ith me one night, an' win ev'y woman in 'e house. I guess 'ey wuz mo' 'an a dozen razahs shahpened faw ol' Albe't 'at night."

"What in the world is a rent-rag?"

"You do n't know what a rent-rag is, misteh? I guess you ain't been out 'round Deahbohn Street ve'y much. You see, misteh, 'ey's quite a numbah o' cullud fam'lies 'at's hahd up 'iss time o' yeah, an' 'ey can't ve'y well come up 'ith 'e rent.' So 'ey have pahties, an' chahge ev'y one someping to come in — ten cents sometimes, o' as much as two bits. 'At's 'e way some of 'em got to do to stand off 'e lan'lohd. Ev'ybody comes in and has good time, an' 'e fam'ly's two or three dollahs to 'e good. Yes, seh, we had some ve'y wahm sessions at 'em rent-rags. 'Ey's sutny good. Take it 'bout two 'clock in 'e mawnin' 'ith all of 'em po'tehs and waitehs kind o' crackin' 'ith Tom gin, I tell you it ain't safe to staht nothin'. 'At's what I say: 'Be good, but do n' staht nothin' 'cuz anything stahted it's goin' 'o finish at 'e hospital, suh's you' bawn.' 'Long 'bout two you got to be caihful whose lady you lay you' hand on. 'Cuz I know. I see Grant Jenkins pull his 'ol bahbeh's friend one night, and begin makin' signs at ol' Gawge Lippincott's brotheh, 'at 'uz visitin' heah f'om In'anapolis, an', mistch, you jus' ought to see Pink come down 'em staihs. O, I guess I was slow, wuz n' I? I did n' wait to walk down. No, seh; I wuz too busy. I jus' fell, 'at's all I done. If 'ey's eveh goin' 'o be any cahvin', misteh, I jus' soon go home an' 'en read 'bout it in 'e papeh nex' mawnin'. Yes, seh; I do n' mind waitin' to find out what 'e finish is."

"You must be associated with a desperate crowd."

"No, seh; 'em boys ain't tough on'y faw a few 'at gets mixed in. I been to some of 'em pahties out theah 'at uz 'e real thing, misteh. Yes, seh; most ev'y one have on 'em dress suits. 'At's wheah they lose me, misteh. Most of of 'em cullud waitehs got to have 'em suits befo' they can wuhk. Ol' Pink shows up 'ith his blue cloze an' he ain't one-two-three. Guess I'll have to be waiteh if I'm goin' 'o be strong out theah. I ain' sayin' a wuhd, but I'm jus' layin' faw a suit of 'em cloze 'at some white gemman's got th'ough usin'. You eveh le' me get a suit of 'em real boys, misteh, an 'ey's nothin' on 'e South Side goin' 'o pass me — no, seh. I'll put some of 'em coffee-cullud waitehs in a trance, 'cuz 'em suits 'ey flash is bad — got grease-spots all down 'e front."

"How would you like to have a suit with silk facing on the lapels?" asked the morning customer.

"Hush, man, hush! Don n' get me to dreamin'."

"I've got a dress-suit you can have if you want it."

"Look out, man! Be caihful! Do n' say it 'less you mean it, 'cuz 'at's jus' what I'm needin'."

"I mean it. I had to buy a new suit a few weeks ago. The old one's up there at the room, and you can have it any time you come for it."

"Misteh, I be theah 'iss aftehnoon ahead o' you, I p'omise you that."

"All right. I do n't know whether it will fit you or not. I think you 're a little larger than I am."

"It's got to fit me, misteh. I need it, an' it's got to fit me. I won'
do a thing 'ith 'at ol' suit nex' Satuhday night, I guess."

"What is it — a rent-rag?"

"No, seh; 'e Sons an' Daughtehs o' Estheh goin' 'o have dance
at Temp'ance Hall. I guess I won' be theah at all."

"O, I see. You are going to execute a social *coup de main.*"

"I'll be wuhse'n 'at, misteh. I'll make 'em cheap waiteh's put on
theah ovehcoats an' go home."

The morning customer wrote his home address on a card.

That evening he found Pink waiting at the front gate. The suit of
evening clothes, with the real silk facing on the coat, was wrapped
up in a newspaper and handed out to the boy, who did fancy
walking steps as he went away, keeping time to his own music.

On the Pride Which Goes Before a Fall

There was a strange face in the corner. Pink was missing.

The morning customer hesitated for a moment, and then he climbed up on the throne and sat in the saggy arm-chair.

"Shine?" asked the new boy.

"No, I want to be manicured," replied the morning customer.

The colored youth stood still and looked at the man in the chair. He seemed to be in doubt.

"Do n' you want no shine?" he asked.

"Of course I want a shine."

Pink's successor settled down on the stool as if in a general collapse, and began to sponge mud from the shoe on the footrest.

He was tall and loose-jointed. His color was that of coffee not yet roasted. The forelock of his kinky hair stood up like a steeple. Instead of a shirt he wore a cotton sweater, which had been white at one time. His brown coast was short for him, and the black braid had been worn away in places. The trousers were a shiny black.

He went at his work slowly and solemnly. The morning customer leaned his elbows on the arms of the chair and studied him. Then he asked: "Where is the boy who was here last week?"

"I dunno."

"Is he sick?"

"I dunno."

"How did you happen to get this job?"

"Well, seh, he did n' show up yes'day mawning'. I guess he's fiahed."

"What's your name?"

"Edwahd Petehs."

"All right, Eddie. Will you just hurry a bit? Your technique is good, but your tempo is bad."

The new boy looked up sleepily and made no response. He

toiled patiently, but the shine which he imparted was nothing more than a dull, metallic burnish.

The morning customer passed upon him and decided that he was tired, wobbly, and uninteresting.

And where was Pink?

Mr. Clifford was not at the shop, so the morning customer applied to Mr. Adams for information. Mr. Adams, who was chewing gum and looking at a colored weekly, did not trouble himself to look up when the question was addressed to him. He smiled in fixed admiration at a noisy cartoon and said, "The old man let him go."

The morning customer went back to his office feeling that a part of his morning had been wasted.

It was about two o'clock in the afternoon when the office-boy came to the door and said, "Colored feller wants to see you."

"A colored fellow! Who is he? What does he want to see me about?"

"I do n't know. He's got one hand wrapped up."

"Well, I can't imagine — tell him to come in."

With hesitating steps William Pinckney Marsh came to the doorway. His overcoat collar was turned up, and one of his hands was bound up in a rude bandage, which was fastened with a large safety-pin. He had a sorrowful gaze. His eyeballs were threaded and bloodshot.

The morning customer repressed an unfeeling inclination to laugh. He put himself on his dignity and asked: "O, it's you, is it, Pink?"

"Yes, seh, jus' some pieces o' me, 'at 's all."

"Sit down."

Pink eased himself down into a chair, shook his head as if in bitterness of spirit, and gave a gusty sigh.

"What's this I hear about you losing your job?" asked the morning customer.

"I'm a good thing, misteh," said Pink, soothing the bandaged hand.

"You do n't seem to be particularly joyous about it. Have you had any trouble?"

"Misteh, I ain' had nothin' else. No use talkin', I stahted out to do too much in one night. I stahted bold, misteh, but I sutny got lost at 'e finish."

"Well, my time is valuable, Pink. If you have any tale of woe, why, go ahead with it."

"Misteh, it 'uz 'at dress-suit you give me. I wanted to be too good, too good."

"Did you go to the ball?"

"'At's wheah I stahted faw, misteh. I stahted all right. I wuz goin' to take 'at Miss Lo'ena Jackson to 'e pahty of 'at Sons an' Daughtehs o' Estheh. I got on 'em cloze you give me, an' I look myse'f oveh an' say: 'O, I guess I'm pooh.' Yes, seh, I wuz too wahm. Stahted out good, on'y I wanted to make flash befo' some of 'em boys 'at hangs out at Mahtin's — yes, seh."

"Martin's being, I presume, a saloon kept by a gentleman of your own color?"

"Yes, seh," said Pink, weakly. "I goes in Mahtin's, an' I see Clay Walkeh an' some mo' boys rollin' 'e bones. I go up to Clay, an' I say· 'What's you' point?' He say: 'Nine.' I say, 'Two bits you seven,' an' he done it. Misteh, I pick up my two frien's an' breathe on 'em an —"

"Look here, Pink," said the morning customer, glancing at the clock on top of the desk, "I have n't time to follow you through the intricacies of a crap game. What happened?"

"Misteh, 'em dice didn't have nothin' but sevens faw me. I win eight dollahs fast as I could pick money up. I could n' quit afteh I got 'at much, not 'ithout takin' chances. Yes, seh, I had on 'em cloze, an' ev'ything comin' my way, an' I could n' get 'em drinks fast enough. Gin an' honey, 'at's what I wuz throwin' in."

"Then you became intoxicated?'

"Misteh, I fawgot Miss Lo'ena Jackson an' 'at pahty. 'Em cloze made me too good. I wuz gamblin' 'ith race-hoss boys an' suah-'nough spohts, an' I would n' let no man pass me."

"How did you hurt your hand?"

"Yes, seh, 'at 's wheah gemman tried to do me 'ith a pokeh."

"That's pleasant. And how did you come to lose your job?"

"Misteh, I woke up 'bout ten 'clock nex' mawnin' on a table in 'at back room at Mahtin's."

"All your money gone, I suppose."

"Do n't ask, man; do n't ask."

"So you did n't show up for work?"

"Yes, seh, 'at 's jus' what I done an' 'ey had 'notheh boy on 'e chaih. Mister Cliffo'd sen' me out of 'e shop, 'cuz he say I wuz n' sobeh yet."

"I expect he was right. What are you going to do now? Have you got another job?"

"No, seh; I'm sutny on 'e edge of 'at cahpet, misteh."

"You remember what I told you about saving your money? If you had a little money in the bank now, you'd be all right."

"Yes, seh, if I had some money in 'e bank, I would n' caih so much to get wuhk right away."

"I expect not. There's no need of working as long as you have a cent anywhere on earth. Well, what are you going to do?"

"Misteh, I want to write letteh to Misteh Cliffo'd, an' say 'at if he'll put me back on 'e chaih, I'll sutny conduc' myse'f as gemman should in a bahbeh-shop."

"Yes, — and what else do you want to tell him?"

"Yes, seh, I say to tell Misteh Cliffo'd 'at I'm a man among men, an' neveh inten' to do no pusson no hahm, and if he hiahs me back in 'at shop I'll sutny g'antee to conduc' myse'f sa'sfacto'y."

"All right."

The morning customer touched a push-button, and a young woman came in from the outer room with a book in her hand.

"Take this," said he, and after the young woman had seated herself he dictated as follows:

Mr. CLIFFORD — Dear Sir: "To err is human; to forgive, divine." Your petitioner beseeches you from a contrite heart to forgive and forget his recent wandering from the straight and narrow path. He admits that, as a result of circumstances which cannot be set forth in this connection, he partook too freely of alcoholic stimulants, and thereby rendered himself incapable of appearing at your establishment at the customary hour to assume the duties allotted to him. Mr. Clifford, remember what the poet says: "Judge not, but rather in your heart let gentle pity dwell."

I am a man among men, and if you should deem it advisable to reinstate me in the responsible position which I held in your tonsorial apartments, I can assure you that I will so conduct myself as to promote your business interests and bring the glad flush of pleasure to the cheek of

"LO'ENA"

your most fastidious patron. Do not condemn a young man for all time because of one offense. Never before, during my entire occupancy of the position at your establishment, did I forget the ancient glory of my race or my own standing as an Afro-American, and allow myself to fall into the clutches of the rum fiend. Now that I have come to a new realization of the scriptural line, "At the last it biteth like a serpent and stingeth like an adder," I am fully determined to abstain from all spirituous, vinous or malt intoxicating liquors, and especially gin and honey.

I am credibly informed that the gentleman who has succeeded me, and who is now making a pitiable attempt to win the favor of the public, is not an artist of any standing, and that his work has been the subject of severe criticism. Therefore, I humbly request that the past be forgotten, and that we soon resume those relations which were productive of pleasure to me and, I am quite sure, of some pecuniary profit to you. I have the extreme honor to subscribe myself, very truly and affectionately,

"Now, when she gets that written out, you can sign it," said the morning customer.

Pink had been listening to the dictation with such consuming interest that his eyes were set and staring, and his lower lip hung down and out like a drooping red petal. When the morning customer spoke to him he blinked and shook his head slowly as if he were coming out of heavy slumber.

"If 'at letteh do n' put me back, it jus' means I can't be put, 'at 's all," said he.

On the Relative Merits of
Great Contemporaries

Three days after the dictation of the letter, the morning customer received a postal-card which read as follows:

Yore letter got me my job back. Old cusstomers always welcom.
Yours truely,
WILLIAM PICKNEY MARSH

He laughed, and sent the card out to his stenographer.

Next morning he did not go to Mr. Clifford's shop. He knew that if he seemed over-willing to promote an intimacy, Pink would no longer hold him in awe.

On the second morning he went to the shop. Pink arose from the corner smiling expectantly, but the morning customer responded with a conservative nod, and climbed into the chair without speaking. He knew that if he encouraged familiarity at this crisis, he might lose his place as an oracle, and certainly he would cease to be a height.

Pink was somewhat abashed by the coolness of his patron. He went to work quietly, and after a while he said: "Well, seh, I'm back heah."

"So I see. I trust it is with the determination to make amends for the past."

"You know me, misteh. Jus' watch me lay low."

"You and Mr. Clifford are once more on friendly terms?"

"My goodness, misteh, jus' like brothehs. Yes, seh, Misteh Cliffo'd say I can have 'iss job jus' long as I keep sobeh. Drink it, misteh? Huh-uh! 'Come on, Pink, an' have someping.' 'No, seh, 'at stuff used me wrong—do n' wan' no mo' of it.'"

"No more gin and honey, eh?"

"Hush, misteh! 'At's bad—bad! Gin an' honey's bad, misteh.

It is sutny smooth bev'age, but it hahms you jus' like 'at five-cent whisky. Ain' got no claws while it's goin' down, misteh, but you get it to wuhkin', an' you want to get right out an' fight yo' own fam'ly. Do n' do thing to you, no, seh."

"When did you get back here?"

"Day befo' yes'day mawnin', misteh. 'At letteh you got up faw me fix it 'ith Misteh Cliffo'd. My goodness, 'at 'uz a wahm boy, suah! Some of 'em wuhds you tossed into Misteh Cliffo'd neveh come out o' no small book, no, seh. 'Em 'uz 'e real tomolleys. Some of 'em too good f' Misteh Cliffo'd, an' he kind o' guesses 'at he's 'e real thing, too."

Just then there was an outbreak at the other end of the room. The barber with the white tie was waving paper money and telling Mr. Adams that he must either "put up or shut up." Mr. Adams appeared to be in a scornful mood. He walked toward his own chair and made a side remark, to the effect that it was a "bluff." Thereupon the barber with the white tie laughed defiantly and put the money back into his pocket.

"What's the matter with those gentlemen?" asked the morning customer.

"Do n't know what 'at is? 'Em wise boys is settlin' 'at fight next week. Yes, seh, 'ey been bettin' jus' like 'at all day yes'day an' to-day, an' I ain't seen no money go up yet. 'Em boys is full o' spohtin' blood."

"Well, what do you think of the fight yourself?"

"Misteh, it's bet'een two of 'em cheap white fightehs, an' it don' make no diff'ence who wins. S'pose Misteh Cliffo'd knock out Misteh Adams — 'at don' show nothin'. It's jus' like goin' into 'at sideshow an' thinkin' you see 'e real suhcus."

"What do you mean by that?"

"You know well 'nough what I mean, misteh — man like you 'at reads all 'bout 'ese boys in 'e papehs. I mean 'ey's one ol' boy 'at can jus' fold 'em up an' lay 'em away as fast as you hand 'em to him, yes, seh."

"Do you mean Sullivan?"

"Listen to you talk! No, seh, I don' mean no John L. I mean 'e wahmest one at eveh wuz — Peteh Jackson."

"O, Peter Jackson? He was a good man."

"Make it betteh 'n good, misteh; make it strongeh. He 'uz 'at ol' teacheh, Peteh wuz, an' all 'em otheh boys had to go to school to 'im. Any time ol' Peteh get licked, all 'em cullud boys 'long Ahmoh Av'nue an' Deahbohn Street sutny goin' 'o stahve. Anybody goin' 'o do Peteh betteh get razah an' a gun."

"I was under the impression that he and Corbett fought a draw once."

"Look heah, misteh! Do n't you know 'bout 'at draw? Peteh had his leg broke an' could n' get at Misteh Cawbett. Peteh even ketch up 'ith 'at pompado' boy — all off, suah! Peteh even push Misteh Cawbett 'ith one of 'em big black hams — Mister Cawbett would n' be lookin' f' no fight 'ith Mr. Fitz now, now, seh. He'd jus' 'bout be gettin' out of 'at hospital."

"Oh, I think you 're prejudiced in favor of Peter on account of his color. He's out of it now."

"Well, seh, if he *is* out of it 'at's mighty good thing faw some of 'ese boy fightehs. 'Cuz if Peteh eveh comes back 'iss way, somebody has sutny got to be eat, yes, seh!"

"Did you ever see Peter?"

"Hush, man! Did I? I took a drink 'ith Misteh Peteh Jackson one day down at Johnson's. You see Peteh walk into 'at place an' ev'y Pullman po'teh an' lunch-room boy jus' drop down on his knees and shake like 'at. Ol' Will Ahbuckle — say, misteh! Ol' Will Ahbuckle he spah 'ith cullud fellow f'om Milwaukee oveh heah on 'e lake front one night, an' he got it all fixed 'ith himse'f 'at he wuz suah-nough p'ize fighteh. One day he wuz stan'in at 'e bah in Johnson's tellin' a lot of 'em cheap yellow boys how to get in 'ith 'at knock-out. My goodness, misteh, he wuz makin' all 'em sassy swings an' uppeh-cuts — oh, he wuz good! All o' sudden 'em boys' eyes kind o' bug out an' some one say: 'Look out, Will, 'at's him now.' 'Who is it?' ol' Will hollehs, swingin' round — bad, you know. Somebody tol' him it wuz Peteh Jackson. My goodness, misteh, you jus' ought to seen — tuhned kind o' white, suah. He neveh said 'notheh wuhd all 'e time Misteh Peteh Jackson 'uz theah. He jus' kep' still an' give him 'at eye. Oscah Jones says Will neveh did get to be as black agen as he wuz 'at day Peteh walked in."

"So you 're not taking much interest in this coming fight?"

"Jus' side-show, misteh, 'at's all. Can't have no suah-'nough p'ize fight 'ithout ol' Peteh bein' theah. Co'se Gawge Dixon's puhty wahm boy, an' 'at Misteh Joe Woolcott ain't so cold, but 'ey 's on'y one hot baby, misteh, an' 'at's Misteh Peteh Jackson f'om Aust'alia."

"You seem to think that the Afro-Americans are invincible."

"How's 'at, misteh?"

"I say, you seem to think that a colored man can't be defeated."

"On'y way to lick cullud man, misteh, is to ketch him on 'e shin."

"On the shin? Does that hurt?"

"Huht, man? My goodness! You see Polk Street coppeh takin' in one of 'em bad boys f'om 'e levee — he do n't hit him on no head. He jus' rap him one 'cross 'e shin an' 'at cullud boy lay down an' yell jus' like he been shot. Cullud boy sutny can't stan' nothin' on his shin. I see cullud boy f'om Palmeh House put on 'e gloves one night 'ith white fellow down heah at Batte'y D, misteh. 'At white man he pound 'at cullud boy on 'e head till his knuckles all broke, an' 'e cullud boy kep' comin' back an' askin' faw mo'. 'En when 'at ref'ee wuz n' lookin', 'at white man spiked 'e cullud boy on 'e shin. Misteh, he could 'nt get 'em gloves off soon 'nough. Yes, seh, misteh, you eveh have any trouble 'ith a cullud boy, you get up as neah to him as you can an' say, ''At's all right, seh, we do n' want no ahgament,' an' 'en you get in hot one on his shin befo' he has time to reach f' anything. You got him licked, suah."

"Well, that's very interesting, but I do n't expect to have any altercations with colored men."

"I don' know, seh. You can't tell, misteh. One of 'em fresh ones come in State Street cah an' set down in you' lap an' you got to notice him. You jus' got to do it."

The morning customer made no response. In a few moments Pink looked up and said:

"Misteh, ah yo' too busy mos' all time to get me up 'notheh letteh?"

"Who is it this time?"

"Yes, seh; 'at lady I tol' you 'bout one day heah."

"I remember. What was her name?"

"Miss Lo'ena Jackson."

'No relation to Peter, eh?"

"No, seh, but she's jus' as wahm."

"This is the girl who expected you to buy a bicycle for her."

"'At's 'e one, misteh. She's been ridin' 'at wheel ev'y night 'iss winteh while she wuz 'sleep. I kind o' queeah myse'f 'ith Lo'ena 'at night I wuz goin' 'o take huh to 'at pahty of 'em Sons an' Daughtehs 'o Estheh. No use talkin'; I need one of 'em hot lettehs to squaih it. I need it bad. If you jus' want to get up someping 'at 'll fix 'at lady, w'y, you know me, seh. I'm a pusson 'at 'peciates any good deed done to me, an' I show any consid'ation possible."

"I'll think it over," said the morning customer, dryly. "I think it's best to keep you on probation for a while."

"Well, seh, you know me, seh," said Pink, as the morning customer arose. "I gen'ally try to be man among men, and you'll find 'at my p'obation is sutny all right. Good mawnin', seh."

On Man's Love of Power and Dominion

Now, although the morning customer did not aspire to become private secretary to Pink, combining the duties of that office with his continuous task as oracle, he felt it to be his bounden duty to compose a letter to Miss Lorena Jackson. He did not attempt to excuse Pink's conduct on the night of the reception given by the Sons and Daughters of Esther, and he admitted to himself that Pink had practiced a confidence game on Miss Jackson by his implied promise to give her a bicycle. Pink was not worthy, that seemed certain, and yet the morning customer forgave him, in that easy charity which enables us to forgive so many sins that are not directly against us. He prepared a letter, and when he had concluded it, he smiled brightly to himself, for he believed the letter to be one of the best things he had written.

At the barber-shop he passed the solicitous Mr. Clifford and his associates, and climbed to the throne, where he waited.

"Can you tell me about the gentleman in charge of this department?" he asked.

"Pink!" shouted Mr. Adams.

"Yes, seh; right heah, seh," came a voice from behind the morning customer, and Pink emerged from the corner pocket, and with his head far back looked at the morning customer from under wavering eyelids.

"You want to keep awake, there," said Mr. Adams very sternly.

"Yes, seh," replied Pink meekly, with a concealed grin. "Good mawnin', misteh."

"Good morning, Mr. Marsh. Have you got time to do a little something to these shoes?"

"Have I got time? Well, you know me, misteh. I ain't heah to ovehlook no friend o' mine, no, seh."

He seated himself in front of the shoe on the foot-rest and asked in a low tone: "You heah Misteh Adams make 'at wahm crack at me?"

"Yes; he seems to be full of authority this morning."

"All of 'em, misteh; ev'y one of 'em thinks he's got to call off f' me, o' else I jus' could n' get along. Misteh Cliffo'd, he's boss; Misteh Adams, he's sup'ntenden'; Misteh Bahclay, he's manageh, an' 'at new bahbeh, he's fo'man. Yes, seh; I'm wuhkin' faw fo' men heah. Misteh Adams got to get back at somebody 'cuz his wife sutny got him tame down. W'y, Mis' Adams come down heah 'bout twice a week an' shake Misteh Adams down f' ev'y cent he's got. Yes, seh; when she gets th'ough 'ith him he's so clean he don' need to take no bath faw month. Yes, seh; he see huh comin' down 'em staihs an' he kind o' tuhns pale an' stahts in to hunt faw what he's got. She won't even leave him no pinch o' change f' cah faih. He got to touch Misteh Cliffo'd to get home. 'At's a fac'."

"Well, every man likes to give orders to some one."

"Suah thing, misteh. I do n' caih what 'ese bahbehs say to me. I jus' want to stay heah till 'em green leaves come out, an' 'en I'm goin' 'o get a chaih o' my own somewheahs. I sutny do n' like to split my good coin 'ith no white man."

"Well, as I've told you a dozen times, if you want to get into business for yourself, you must begin and save your money."

"Yes, seh; jus' you watch me. If ev'ything comes good, misteh, 'long 'bout nex' August I'll be eatin' watehmelon an' smokin' cigahs when 'em white bahbehs is settin' 'round heah fightin' flies."

"'Hope springs eternal in the human breast; man never is, but always to be, blest,'" observed the morning customer.

"O, I guess 'at's pooh, ain't it? 'At's bad writin'. Gi' me to me agen, misteh. 'At's one I want to pass to ol' Gawge Lippincott."

"You look it up yourself. You can find it in any book of poetry."

"Hush, man! I know who wrote 'at, an' you can't make me believe nothin' else — no, seh."

"Well, who wrote it?"

"Misteh, I know who done it. You done it, yo'se'f — ain't 'at so?"

"How did you suspect it?" asked the morning customer, laughing.

"Misteh, you can't fool me all 'e time. On'y man could do it.

"MISTEH ADAMS"

What is it — 'Hope in 'e human breast'? Goodness, if I could jus'
toss off few like 'at I'd have some of 'em State Street rascals jumpin'
out of 'e windows."

"Speaking of your social affiliations, have you succeeded as yet
in effecting a reconciliation with Miss Jackson?"

Pink looked up, and his big eyes were blinking gravely. But
the morning customer kept a straight face. It served his purpose
to remain calm and unconcerned when he was hurling these big
words.

Pink chuckled away down in his lungs as he folded the flannel.

"'At Miss Lo'ena Jackson use me jus' like man she neveh seen.
I passed huh on 'e street otheh day, an' she begin' lookin' fo' some
one at secon' sto'y window. She kep' lookin' at 'e window, an'
neveh see me at all — jus' gi' me 'at 'brush-by' sign, an' no mo'.
When it comes to playin' faw huh, misteh, I'm jus' a deuce in a
duhty deck — 'at's all."

"Do you think you could reinstate yourself in her affections if
you were to write to her?"

"Misteh, she's keen. Yes, seh, she's took a lot of 'at co'n f'om 'em
cullud boys, an' she's beginnin' to give ev'y man 'at bad look when
he tells huh how good she is. Mistch, you can't feed it to 'em f'-
eveh. No, seh, 'ey sutny get wise afteh while."

"Did n't you say you wanted me to get up a letter to send to her?"

"Misteh, I tell you one thing — if I eveh land 'at baby back on 'e
resehvation I jus' got to have one of 'em wahm lettehs like you sent
to Misteh Cliffo'd. No talk 'at I can swing is eveh goin' 'o move
'at lady; no, seh."

"Well, I'll tell you, Pink, I have concocted an epistle here which
may act as a solvent on her heart. I'll read it to you, and if you
think it's all right, you can send it."

"All right, misteh? All right? It jus' could n' he'p but be all
right. Watch out faw 'em white bahbehs. If 'ey see you readin' 'at,
ev'y one of 'em goin' 'o rubbeh, sauh."

"You do n't want them to hear it, eh?"

"Goodness, misteh! I should say not. I got trouble 'nough heah
now 'ithout havin' all 'ese smaht boys askin' me 'bout 'at guhl
ev'y ten minutes."

"All right. I'll read it low. Are you ready?"

"Misteh, I can't heah it too soon."

The morning customer made sure that the barbers were out of hearing distance. They were bunched at the other end of the room, talking about things to eat.

He leaned over and read, and during the reading Pink was so absorbed that he simply rubbed the shoe in a slow and absent-minded way.

"To Miss Jackson, the Hebe of her Sex.

"My Dearest Miss Jackson: Seated here today, in my boudoir, my thoughts revert to these beautiful lines:

> " 'You may break, you may shatter
> The vase, if you will,
> But the scent of the roses
> Will cling round it still.'

"You may project me into ethereal space, Miss Jackson, but you cannot induce me to forget those whilom hours when yu and I were wont to

> " '. . . . breathe out the tale
> Beneath the milk-white thorn."

"I have been meditating to-day upon the cruelties of Fate. Only a few days ago we were bound together by the reciprocal bonds of Love's young dream. To-day you scorn the sable Lothario who, figuratively speaking, prostrates himself at the shrine of Beauty and begs the slight meed of forgiveness, even if he can never again bask in the dazzling effulgence of your incandescent society. Something tells me that a dark cloud has come between us. Who can it be that would seek to uproot the budding tendrils of Platonic love and plant in place thereof the noxious weeds of venomous hatred? Surely these words will convey to your susceptible woman's heart some approximate conception of the mental anguish which racks my sturdy frame. The birds, sweet harbingers of spring, will soon be disporting themselves in the trees, ever and anon bursting forth into joyous melody.

> " 'Come, gentle spring,
> Etheral mildness, come.'

"In fancy I had pictured many glad days during this period of the earth's awakening. I had thought that we would go forth beside the babbling brook and listen to the soughing wind whisper its message to our eager souls. I await a token which will bring me, palpitating with love, to make amends for all the sad and bitter past. I beg to subscribe myself, very apologetically."

Pink made motions with his hands, as if he were recovering consciousness.

"'At's 'e wahmest eveh! he exclaimed. "Misteh, you send 'at to Miss Lo'ena Jackson an' she'll be wuhkin' on it a yeah f'om now. Yes, seh, she'll be settin' up nights spellin' out 'em long ones."

"You will observe that I said nothing about your being intoxicated on the night when you should have taken her to the party," said the morning customer, folding the letter.

"O, I guess you ain't wise, neetheh! Misteh, I neveh could n' 'splain to huh 'bout 'at night I got good on gin an' honey. You done right. Jus' let 'at go. Wait'll she gets 'at letteh. My goodness, misteh! She'll be waitin' out on 'em cah tracks faw me to get home."

Pink took hold of the letter as if it were an explosive. He promised to mail it immediately.

On Revenge

"Misteh, I'm a good ol wagon, but I done broke down, jus' like it says in 'at song," began Pink Marsh.

"What's the matter now?"

"You know 'at letteh you got up faw me to sen' to Miss Lo'ena Jackson."

"Yes. Did you sent it?"

"'At's what I done, misteh, an' it was too good. Yes, seh, it was so high she could n' reach it."

"You seemed to think that letter was going to placate her."

"Yes, seh, I kind o' s'posed she 'uz wahm enough to 'peciate suah-thing letteh, but I'm tellin' you she don' know yet what 'at letteh's about. I'm done 'ith 'at lady. She mus' n' come neah me no mo'. I jus' hope huh an' 'at Gawge Lippincott gets mah'ied, 'cuz I can see him out stealin' coal right now. 'At Gawge Lippincott wants to keep in nights, too, misteh. Ev'y night he wants to lock 'e dooh an' go to bed, 'cuz I tell you he ain't safe. If he eveh gets on 'e same street 'ith me, I'm li'ble to cloud up an' rain on him. Yes, seh, people be pickin' up dahk meat all oveh 'e South Side."

"Well, well, you are warlike this morning."

"He's 'e one 'at done it, misteh. He tol' huh ev'ything he knows 'bout me. Yes, seh, he's been knockin' good an' plenty, an' if he ain't caihful I'll fly down an' bite a piece out o' him. When I get th'ough 'ith him, people come up an' say, 'My goodness, 'at ain't Gawge Lippincott,' an' 'en 'ey all go to lookin' faw his face."

"Well, I hope it will not be as serious as that," said the morning customer. "What's the matter. Did n't the girl answer the letter?"

"Yes, seh, misteh; she sent answeh, an' she did n' do thing to Misteh William Pickney Mahsh, neetheh. W'y, misteh, I could read Gawge Lippincott in 'at letteh jus' same as if his pickchah on it. Yes, seh, misteh, 'ey'll be a fune'al on Ahmoh Av'nue, an' ol' Gawge Lippincott won't heah no music. 'At's right, seh. I'm a man among men, an' when any punkin-cullud houn' goes suhculatin' 'roun' spoilin' my cha'cteh, his friends want to begin speakin' faw caih'ages right away, 'cuz 'ey got to make a trip to 'at graveyahd, suah."

"What did she say in the letter?"

Pink turned around to see if the white barbers were watching him, and then he drew a crumpled envelope from his hip pocket and passed it up to the morning customer.

The letter had been written with pencil and was blurred and smeary, but the morning customer made it out to be as follows:

"Mr. Marsh, Esq. Dear Sir. Probly you think you can cause me to feel diferent about the eve when you was to be my company at the ball which is not so. Oh I think you had better try to write one more letter and then stop it is not because I wanted to go with you as it is not the case you know that I have gentlemen friends who do not get so drunk when they are to take you that evry one hears about it Ha, Ha, so you see I know a sertain person said Oh why do you waist a 2 cent stamp on him but I said to let him know he ain't so smart after all.

Yours truly,
"Lorena Jackson."

When the morning customer had finished reading, he shook his head, choked down an inclination to laugh, and said: "Well, Pink, she is certainly a wonder."

Pink looked up and caught the morning customer grinning, and then he began to laugh.

"Misteh, 'at guhl ain' got no mo' ej'cation 'an 'at stove oveh theah," he said. "She can jus' put on one of 'em regulah Mis' Potteh Palmeh fronts when it comes to settin' up an' talkin', but when you make huh put it down on papeh, w'y, you got 'uh lost, suah. 'Em wuhds ain't right, ah they, misteh?"

"Some of them might be improved upon."

"Look at 'at letteh! Looks like some one been th'owin coal dust at 'e papeh."

"She certainly conveys the impression that you are *persona non grata*."

"O, man! 'At's a new one, suah! At's faw'eign, ain't it? Wha's 'e defmition?"

"Well, it means that you 're not in it."

"'At's right, misteh. I might jus' well teah up my tickets now, but I'm goin' o' be good loseh. I make no holleh, misteh. She 'uz neveh mo 'n thuhty to one shot noways, an' I on'y played couple o' dollahs on 'uh."

"You never gave her that bicycle you promised, then, did you?"

Pink stopped work and spluttered with mirth. Then he said: "Misteh, it ain' no good way to do. It ain't right to fool 'em 'at way, no, seh. Lo'ena lose huh wheel now, suah. I'll have to use 'at bike sto'y on some otheh lady. Lo'ena ain't 'e on'y good thing on Deah-bohn Street. 'Ey'll be many a wahm child standin' at 'e front gate an' waitin' f' Misteh Mahsh nex' summeh. I'm like 'at boy in 'e oct'oon show. 'All coons looks alike to me.'"

"Oh, yes, that's a song. I think I've heard it."

"Yes, an' 'at's a pooh one, too. 'At's bad. Le's see — 'O, all' — no, 'at's too high. 'All coons looks' — 'at's 'bout right."

With his eyes dreamily half-closed, Pink sang as follows, using the soft pedal:

"All a-coons looks alike to me;
I got a new beau, you see,
An' he's- a jus' as good to me
As you, niggeh, eveh daihed to be,
He's sutny a-good to me;
He spen's his-a money free.
I do n' like you a-nohow;
All-a coons looks alike to me."

"You have quite a voice," said the morning customer.

"Hush, misteh, you did n' know I belong to 'at Elect'ic Quahtette. My goodness! Me an' Grant Williams an' Oscah Wellington an' Fred Bahnett. Oh-h-h, when we hit 'at sassy chohd in 'Ev'nin' by Moonlight,' wheah it comes, ''Ey would set all night an' listen-n-n-n' — I guess 'at's bad. We get in a minoh 'at'd coax a buhd out of a cage. You ought to see Fred use 'at guitah. Yes, she, he sutny does things to it. Yes, seh, we sung in 'e campaign — on'y one night we got too fah west. Cullud man got no business goin' on otheh side of 'e riveh. We all went oveh to meetin' on 'e Wes' Side an' sing 'em wahm 'publican songs, an we 'uz good. We did n' think it, misteh — we knowed it. We knowed 'ey wuz none better. Jus' we come out, misteh, bing! brickbat right th'ough ol' Fred Bahnett's guitah. Mo'n

CIVIL RIGHTS

a thousan' I'ishmen afteh us, misteh; 'at's right. You talk 'bout cullud men havin' bad feet; you ought to see us run 'at night — Mahsh
in 'e lead, Wellington close secon', Williams and Bahnett neck-an'-
neck, two lengths behind. We broke all recohds — we had to do it.
You think 'ey eveh get us back on 'e Wes' Side? Huh-uh! We know
ouah business."

"You 've got as much right over there as any one has."

"Co'se! Suah! But we ain' goin' oveh no mo' when 'em people's
all het up 'bout pol'tics. 'At's like 'e cullud man oveh in 'e jail. His
lawyeh comes in to see him, an' he says to 'e cullud man, ''Ey
can't put you in jail faw what you done,' an' 'e cullud man says,
'I know 'ey can't, Misteh Lawyeh, but I'm in heah jus' 'e same.'
'At 's 'e way 'ith us, misteh. We got mo' rights 'an anybody, but
it sutny ain't safe to use 'em."

On Independence in Politics

About a week after the morning customer had read the letter from Miss Lorena Jackson, he made another visit to Mr. Clifford's shop. Pink was very happy and explained that as soon as he had paid off a few small debts he expected to open an account in a savings bank. When he had finished cleaning the morning customer's shoes, preparatory to spreading the first layer of dressing, a tall Negro came down the stairway and put his head in at the door.

"Misteh Mahsh heah?" he asked.

Mr. Clifford, the potentate of the shop, was rubbing a quinine tonic into the thin fuzz belonging to a fat man whose jowls lapped down on the napkin and whose eyes were wide open from the zest of the occasion. At brief intervals he groaned with enjoyment, for it is a fact that having one's head rubbed is a pure and noble pleasure on which the gods have set no high price. Between these groans the fat man advanced his views on the subject of tariff legislation. Every opinion was warmly seconded by Mr. Clifford, who was fully able to think tariff and rub the fat man's head, both at the same time.

The interruption of the tariff discussion seemed to annoy Mr. Clifford. He did not condescend to answer the question put to him. He simply made an inclination of the head toward the remote corner in which Pink and the morning customer were having their quiet session.

"Good mawning, Pink," said the visitor, advancing briskly, and trailing a small bamboo cane on the floor.

"How do, Gawge," replied Pink, as he looked up at the visitor, and then, through some mysterious influence which directs the happiness of Afro-American souls, both of them began to shake with laughter.

The so-called "Gawge" was rather tan-colored. A small allot-
ment of freckles gave his face a rusty tinge, while the kinks of
his hair and mustache were touched with auburn. He wore a high
stiff hat with a narrow rim, a suit of navy blue, which had become
spotted black here and there by usage, and the morning customer
made particular note of his scarfpin, which was a large owl's head,
carved of bone and having knobby glass eyes.

"I s'pose you know 'bout ouah goin' to puhfeck an ohganization
to-night," said "Gawge."

"'At meetin', you mean?" asked Pink.

"It's 'specially desiahed by Misteh Milleh 'at we get a good
'tendance at McCahty's Hall to-night. You be suah an' come an'
exuht yo' infloonce to get all 'e boys out. It's goin' to be called
'Milleh In'epen'en' Cullud Votehs League.' I'm sec'eta'y, an'
nachu'lly I feel 'sponsible. Misteh Milleh re'lizes ouah infloonce
an' he's goin' to be ve'y lib'al."

"Yes, seh, Gawge, I'll be on hand."

"Well, I got to be goin' oveh county buildin' an' see a gem'man.
Smoke a cigah, Pink?"

So saying, "Gawge" drew a very pale cigar from his pocket and
handed it to Pink, and then he went out, still trailing his cane over
the tiling.

"Who's that — a friend of yours?" asked the morning customer.

"Who, him? He's 'e boy 'at stahted pol'tics. He's 'e one 'at says
who is an' who ain't. Did you kind o' notice how he flash in an'
flash out? He knows mo' 'bout pol'tics 'an Gen'al Grant eveh did.
When ol' Gawge dies 'ey won't be no mo' pol'tics, no seh."

"What's his name?"

"'At's 'e on'y Gawge 'at eveh happened — Gawge Lippincott."

"George Lippincott? Why, he's the man you were going to kill,
is n' he?"

"Look at him, misteh. I could n' kill good thing like 'at."

"Why, it was n't a week ago that you told me that the first time
you saw him you intended to annihilate him — simply slaughter
him in cold blood."

Pink chuckled aloud and wagged his head knowingly. "Mus n'
kill Gawge now," he said. "We both eatin' out of 'e same pan, yes,

seh. I 'uz goin' 'o do Gawge mo' hahm 'an any man eveh had done to him, but 's no use now, misteh. Gawge is wheah I am now. 'At Lo'ena Jackson toss him a mile higheh 'an she give it to me. She got a new face in 'e pahlah now, suah. Gawge an' me's shahpenin' razahs on 'e same hone 'iss week. Hen'y Clahk's 'e man 'at 's got to be took off 'e map. He's 'e hot papa oveh at Lo'ena's house 'iss week."

"Do you mean to say that Mr. Lippincott has received his congé?"

"No, seh, I do n' know 'bout no conjay, but he sutny got 'e mahble h'aht f'om little Miss Lo'ena. She can' no mo' see wheah he comes in now an' if he'd neveh been. Yes, seh, she fawgets wheah she met him. She do n't even know his name. W'y, misteh, if me an' ol' Gawge go up 'e street togetheh an' she meet us, she say, 'My goodness! Town's jus' full o' strangehs to-day.' 'At's how well she likes us, misteh."

"How did Mr. Lippincott happen to lose his standing?"

"Hen'y Clahk done it. Hen'y's swell lookeh an' got a con talk 'at'd win most any lady. He's po'teh on Pullman cah, an' he jus' land in heah otheh day f'om long piece o' wuhk in p'ivate cah — been way out West. You know, misteh, pahty o' white gem'men out in cah 'at way gen'ally ve'y lib'al 'ith a po'teh 'at knows how to use 'em. I guess Hen'y ain't smooth o' nothin', neetheh! Goodness, misteh, he can brush a man an' bow an' say 'Ev'ything sa'sfacto'y, seh?' an' 'e man jus' got to hand him money. Pahty out two o' three weeks like 'at, an' when 'ey come in ev'y gem'man give 'e po'teh much as five o' ten dollahs 'piece. Ol' Hen'y land in heah 'ith a roll 'at made me an' Gawge Lippincott look like a couple o' dahk lobstehs. Money in ev'y pocket, misteh; p'fume'y on his cloze, an' smokin' 'at long kind 'at you neveh get f' no nickel — no, seh. He meet Lo'ena an' say, 'Miss Jackson, may I espec' 'e honah of givin' you some soda-wateh?' o' someping like 'at, an' 'en he flash 'at bundle o' papeh money. Oh-h-h-h, I guess not! I s'pose she did n' nail him! Wha' d' you s'pose, misteh? Ol' Hen'y loosens up an' buys huh watch. Gawge Lippincott go 'round 'at ev'nin' to see huh, an' she send out wuhd 'at if he do n' go 'way she'll set 'e dogs on him. Gawge can feed 'em nice talk, misteh, but he sutny went into 'e

"GUS MILLEH"

fence soon as Hen'y showed up an' begin to make good 'ith his coin. Lo'ena's like all of 'em, misteh; she's lookin' faw 'e boy 'at'll let go f' theatehs an' jew'lery. When Hen'y give up 'at gol' watch, 'at 'uz when Gawge Lippincott splosh into 'e mud. He'll luhn, misteh, he'll luhn. I'm jus' waitin' faw Hen'y Clahk's finish now. Jus' soon as he uses las' strippeh of 'at roll an' do n' put up nothin' 'cept sayin' how he loves huh, she'll find out 'at he ain't propeh comp'ny, an' ol' Hen'y'll be out on 'e road makin' up loweh seven and guessin' why."

"I'm afraid you're a pessimist as regards the gentle sex."

"I'm wuhse 'an 'at, misteh. I'm an Ind'ian on 'iss heah guhl game. I won't stan' f' nothin' no mo'."

"Well, I must say that you and Mr. Lippincott are bearing up very bravely under your affliction. Mr. Lippincott seems to be finding surcease from his grief in the exciting field of politics."

"Misteh, I wish you'd used someping like 'at when Gawge 'uz in heah. Gawge thinks he's ve'y strong on 'em big wuhds, an' I jus' like to steeh him 'genst some one 'at could make him look foolish. Did you heah 'e kind he 'uz passin' to me in heah?"

"Yes, he seemed to be quite a talker."

"He's a wahm talkeh, an' 'at's all he can do, misteh. Gawge thinks he's 'e whole thing in pol'tics out in ouah wahd, an' nobody likes to wake him up. He's goin' 'o make Gus Milleh aldehman — 'at's what he told Misteh Milleh, an' Misteh Milleh he thinks 'at Gawge got 'e whole cullud vote inside of 'at blue vest. I know betteh. If Gus Milleh wants to land me he betteh come an' see me himse'f. What he does faw ol' Gawge Lippincott ain't helpin' me none — no, seh. Cullud man's 'e real thing 'long 'bout spring 'lection, an' any man 'at gets me to holle'in' faw him has sutny got to use me good. Gawge Lippincott do n't own nobody but himse'f. I'll smoke ol' Gawge's cigars 'at Gus Milleh pays faw, but when it comes to castin' my ballot, seh, as an Ameh'can cit'zen, Gawge Lippincott an' no otheh cullud man goin' o' tell me how to vote — no, seh. I'm faw any man 'at does 'e most faw me — yes, seh."

On the Selection of Apparel

"O, man! I guess you picked 'at out o' some ash-bah'el!" exclaimed Pink Marsh as the morning customer seated himself on the throne and spread the new spring overcoat so that he would not sit on it.

"What are you talking about? O, I see — the coat. Is it all right?"

"No, seh, it's bad — all ragged 'roun' 'e edges, do n't fit in back. 'At's a pooh coat. Goodness! Do n' eveh take it off when yo' in heah, 'cuz if you do, you lose it to me. I jus' need one of 'em shawt cream-cullud boys to make me good. I do n't steal, misteh, but I sutny could use 'at coat."

"Well, I'm glad you like it. It's always a satisfaction to have one's dress approved by a gentleman of taste and discrimination."

"Hush, man, do n't lift me too high. It ain't ev'y cullud boy 'at gets 'at lang'age used on him, is it?"

"No, sir, that is a special eulogium."

"I jus' see 'at one when it go past me. 'Logeum' — 'logeum' — misteh, you got a new one to toss at me ev'y time you come in heah, an' none of 'em ain't so wuhse. 'At's a fact, seh. Some is wahmeh 'an othehs, but ev'y one of 'em smokes."

"That is very kind of you to say so."

"I guess you do n' know how to use cullud pusson good, neetheh. W'y, misteh, some days afteh you come in heah an' give me 'at kind o' convehsation, I feel 'at if I had mo' ej'cation I would n' be rubbin' no man's shoes, no, seh. I'd be lawyeh o' someping like 'at."

"Well, do n't you worry too much. You're probably doing more business than half of the lawyers."

" 'At's all right, misteh, but I'd like to be one of 'em boys 'at gets up an' says, 'Misteh judge an' gem'men of 'iss ju'y, it is p'ivilege faw me to 'peciate yo' 'tention in regahds to 'iss subjec' an' to — "

"Well, do n't forget that you are supposed to be shining those shoes," said the morning customer.

"WATCH ME LAY LOW"

Pink had become so interested in his majestic impersonation of the lawyer addressing the jury that he had laid down his brushes, put one hand on his chest, and extended the other in a sweeping gesture.

When the morning customer interrupted his speech, he suddenly collapsed into laughter and rocked about on his stool, until the morning customer, who seldom gave way to mirth, began to chuckle out of sympathy.

Pink returned to his work on the shoe, but he was still seized with occasional spasms of laughter, and the big yellow-white balls of his eyes were wet with genuine tears.

"It's rather warm in here this morning," observed the morning customer, after Pink had simmered down to his normal gravity, "but I'm afraid to take off this coat after what you said."

"It's all right if you watch it, misteh, but you sutny mus' watch it. I on'y got one kick comin' on 'at coat, misteh."

"Yes — and what's that?"

"Yes, seh, if yo' goin' 'o kill 'em dead, you ought to have some of 'at satin down 'e front. 'Lonzo Williams, down on Twent'-sevem Street, got one of 'em satin kind, so wahm it melts snow right off 'e sidewalk when 'e walks past. People got to put on 'em smoked glasses to look at ol' 'Lonzo when he comes out 'ith 'at coat, suah. Yes, seh, it's kind o' cullah of cana'y buhd, all 'cept down 'e front, an' theah it's blue satin. Oh-h-h-h, I guess it ain't wahm o' nothin'! Got puhl buttons 'bout 'e size of five-cent pie. 'Lonzo come 'long Ahmoh Av'nue 'ith 'at coat on, an' you see 'em, old an' young, misteh, leavin' theah homes to follow him. Yes, seh, he got to tuhn 'round an' yell at 'em to make 'em go back in 'e houses and leave him alone. Yes, seh, ol' 'Lonzo put 'e price o' many a shave into 'at coat."

"Why don't you get one like it, if it gives a man such a standing?"

"My goodness, misteh! 'em coats do n' grow on bushes. No, seh, you sutny got to wave money in front of a tailah befo' he hands you anything like 'at. W'y do n't I get one! I can jus' answeh questions like 'at all day. Ask me some mo'. Ask me why I do n' buy 'at Lake-Front Pahk an' move it out on Deahbohn Street. Misteh, I could n' even buy one of 'em sassy buttons."

"Well, you know what I've been telling you for three months. Save your money. Put away a little something every week, and you'll be surprised to find how it accumulates."

"'At's no lie, misteh, what you tellin' me now. I'll be sup'ised, suah 'nough, if I eveh find any money 'cumulatin' in my cloze. I thought Misteh McKinley get in down at Washin'ton kind o' move mattehs some— kind o' push a little coin towahds me, but do n' seem to, seh."

"Well, of course, if you go and play your money against policy, McKinley can't help you any. What did you count on? Did you think that after McKinley got in he'd send you some money every week? The only way in which McKinley could help you would be to come here and have his shoes shined."

"Well, co'se, misteh, I did n' 'spect to get anything 'less I went out faw it, but I 'uz hopin' I'd have mo' luck afteh Misteh McKinley got to be presiden'.'"

"Yes, you probably thought he might help you catch something at policy. Suppose you did win twenty, thirty, or even fifty dollars at policy. What good would it do you? You'd go out to spend the money, and the chances are that you'd lose your job here. Then where would you be? You'd be out of money and out of a job. I suppose you'd come around to me again and want me to write another letter to Mr. Clifford to get you back into this job."

Pink listened seriously enough until the morning customer had concluded, and then he shook his head and gave way to internal laughter. He made no sound, but his shoulders lifted now and then. He looked up at the morning customer with a moist grin, and said: "No, seh, I fool you, misteh. I would n' waste no good coin on 'em cullud people no mo'. No, seh; I take 'at money an' I make myse'f good. — 'at's what I'd do. See heah, misteh — one o' 'em stiff white hats 'ith a soft top, kind o' pushed in, an' black band 'round it, un'e'stand! Co'se I would n' have no patent-leatheh shoes — I s'pose not. 'Ese shahp boys, 'ith yellow tops. Pants — kind o' buff-cullud. Coat! O, say, misteh, I do n' s'pose I'd have one 'ith stripes, would I? No braid 'long edges, neetheh. O, man! I'd be 'e wahmes' thing 'at eveh come up undeh 'at Twelf' Street vi'duc'. I would'n do thing but jus' walk up an' down in front o' Miss Lo'ena Jackson's house an' say: 'Woman, see what you missed.'"

"You'd have to get a cane with a silver dog's-head, would n't you?" suggested the morning customer.

"I'm buyin' it now, misteh; I'm buyin' it now."

"And a white silk cravat with gold horseshoe on it!"

"Misteh, you sutny got to stop 'at; I can't see yo' shoe."

"Then you want a diamond ring and a double watch-chain with a cameo charm, and a spotted handkerchief with musk on it, and a pair of yellow gloves and — "

"Man alive! Do n' say no mo'! I'm so dopey now I can't finish yo' shoe. You sutny got to stop."

"How about smoking a ten-cent cigar?"

"Make it fifteen, misteh, 'ith a yellow papeh 'round it. Put about fo' hund'ehd dollahs in my cloze while yo' at it. Goodness, I sutny am havin' good time to-day."

When the morning customer went away, Pink was just as happy as though he had bought the clothes.

On the Transference of Affections

The morning customer had heard of men losing weight and drooping away to melancholy through disappointment in love, but he observed that Pink was too much of a philosopher to keep company with grief. The boy gave up Lorena Jackson with no sigh of regret. He no longer talked of her.

One day the morning customer, who wished to learn if Pink had a secret sorrow, said in the most casual way:

"I have n't heard you speak of your lady friend lately."

"She ain' no frien' o' mine no mo' — 'at lady, you mean. Some day when she's washin' faw livin' to keep some cheap cullud hound in smokin'-tobacco, you see Misteh William Pinckney Mahsh takin' his wash 'round to huh an' say: 'Woman, if yo do n' get 'iss bundle ready by to-moh'ow night, I take my wuhk somewheahs else, an' you all stahve to death.' Yes, seh, I'll see 'e day, misteh, when 'at piece o' p'oud flesh'll be doin' up my collahs faw me."

"You should n't be so bitter. You seemed to think at one time that Miss — what's her name?"

"Miss Lo'ena Jackson, yes seh."

"Well, you seemed to think at one time that Miss Jackson was an amphibious sort of a girl."

"Misteh, I seen a new stah in 'e sky, an' it shines brighteh an' eveh you see 'at ninety-poun' lady. Le' me tell you, misteh. She ain't so 'phibious as some othehs. 'Ey's a big crop of 'em on 'e South Side, an' if you lose one you suah find anotheh waitin' faw you 'round 'e cawneh."

"I see — just as good fish in the sea as ever were caught."

"Jus' as good fish, misteh, but you sutny do need a little bait. 'Ey won' bite at no bait hook. Yes, seh, you can ketch tuhtle 'ith a piece o' string, misteh, but you got to use fresh bait to land a goggle-eye. An' you got to pull when 'at cohk goes undeh, o' little Miss Goggle-Eye up stream an' took yo' bait 'long 'ith huh."

"Well, you are decidedly figurative this morning."

" 'At's so, misteh, I got it all figgahed out. Man get stung three o' fo' times an' he gets wiseh, no mistake, seh. I'm lookin' f' no mo' ladies 'at's afteh bikes. I'm wantin' 'em, misteh, 'at if you give 'em a few peppehmints an' stan' faw cahfaih, 'ey think they bein' used good. Yes, seh. I kind o' got one snaihed out now, an' I sutny won't spoil 'uh by talkin' jew'lery to 'uh, cuz when you staht 'em in strong you got to make good all 'e time, o' you come to bad finish."

"You've given up all hopes of reconciliation with Lorena, then, have you?"

"Misteh, 'at lady's jus' 'e same to me as day befo' yes'day. She couldn' coax me back to huh, even if she use sugah."

"How about chicken? Suppose she luvited you over to her house to eat chicken?"

"Misteh, I might fool 'ith any chicken she set out," and Pink shook with laughter; "but she couldn' neveh tie me down in 'at pa'lah agen, faw I'm tellin' you I know all 'bout 'at lady's style. You know what she done to Hen'y Clahk? I tol' you 'bout Hen'y Clahk, didn' I?"

"Is he the Pullman porter that cut you and George Lippincott out?"

"Yes, seh, 'at's 'e one. You know he loosen up an' buy 'at gold watch faw Lo'ena. He 'uz 'e hot papa f' 'bout two weeks, an' 'en he went broke. Afteh 'at he begin usin' talk on huh same as ol' Gawge Lippincott. Jus' soon as Hen'y couldn' p'oduce no mo', she find out 'at he's tellin' bad sto'ies 'bout huh cha'cteh, an' she goin' 'o have him cahved by light fellow 'at wuhks in a club. When ol' Hen'y went back on his cah he uz stripped so clean he couldn' change dollah faw man 'at wanted to give him quahteh. 'At's what 'at long-waisted fai'y done to Hen'y Clahk. Misteh, she's sutny a quick finisheh. I'm 'bout 'e on'y boy she neveh sunk 'e hooks into. I kep' huh guessin' 'bout 'at bisickle she 'uz goin' 'o get. I s'pose she likes me, do n't she? She got 'at yellow waiteh now. Yes, seh, if he gets his pay in aftehnoon, you can sutny gamble 'at she's he'pin' him spend it in 'e ev'nin' — an' any time he's slow in comin' up, I can jus' see him huntin' f' new place."

"Well, do I understand you to say that you have a new — young lady?"

"Misteh, I can't say I got huh faw suah, becuz I get 'at con so often befo' 'at I'm slow to say what's mine till 'e race is oveh an' all tickets paid, but it sutny looks as if 'at Miss Belle Hopkins jus' look all 'round an' 'en couldn' see nobody else but Misteh William Pinckney Mahsh. She's whispehed it to me, misteh, 'at if she lose me, ev'ything sutny off, but ol' Misteh Wise Pink, he's huhd 'at talk befo'. I ain't makin' no claims, misteh, 'til I see somebody try to land huh 'way f'om me. 'En I can tell if she's goin' o' stick. Any hoss can win, misteh, if he's got 'e track to himse'f, but you bring out ol' hoss numbeh two, an' 'e one 'at picks 'em up oftenes' an' sets 'em down fah apaht is 'e one 'at you want to put yo' money on."

"What kind of a looking girl is Belle?"

"Betteh 'n 'at, misteh. She's betteh 'n yo' guessin' she is. Yes, seh, she's got mo' feathehs 'an any otheh blackbuhd 'at eveh flew 'long Deahbohn Street, an' she got mo' style in huh walk in one minute 'an 'at half-stahved Lo'ena Jackson eveh had in all huh life. My goodness, misteh, Belle walk jus' like she 'uz takin' last chance at 'e cake, an' had a bad lady to beat out. She's win in mo' n' one walk, an she'd be on 'e stage walkin' long befo' 'iss, on'y huh motheh's ve'y strong Meth'dis' an' do n' like none of 'em pasamala steps. No, seh, Belle can't do none of 'at 'hand on yo' head an' let yo' mind go free' while Mis' Hopkins 'round. Mis' Hopkins got mo' 'ligion 'an she can use. I 'uz down at 'e house otheh ev'nin', an' ol' Mamma Hopkins she kind o' sized me oveh 'e tops of 'em specticles, an' say: 'Misteh Mahsh, do you 'tend chuhch?' I say: 'Yes, umdeed, Mis' Hopkins; I jus' soon think o' losin' a meal as ovehlookin' suhvis.' 'En she say: 'What chuhch do you 'tend, Misteh Mahsh?' an' I say, 'I go out Thuhty-fift' Street, 'cuz 'e preacheh out theah most sutny preach wahm suhmon.' She kind o' look at me an' shake 'uh head. Yes, seh, I'll have to holleh some night befo' I'm strong 'ith ol' Mis' Hopkins. I'll jus' have to go down to 'at chuhch an' drown out Misteh Preacheh Fehguson befo' Mis' Hopkins eveh believe I got 'ligion."

"Yes, Pink, I suppose you are going to add hypocrisy to your other sins," said the morning customer.

BELLE

"No, seh, misteh, 'at ain' no 'poc'asy. I get comvuhted ev'y time I go to chuhch, but on week-days I sutny is what Brotheh Fehguson call a wande'in' sheep. I sutny wandeh when I get 'way wheah I can't heah 'at music."

"Well, perhaps Belle will convert you."

"Hush, man! 'At Belle's a hot tomolley. She no mo' got 'at Meth'dis' 'ligion 'an you have — no, seh. She'd ratheh push huh feet oveh floo' 'at had sand on it. She's got bad feet. She do n' know what to do 'ith 'em feet at all. Shall I kind o' touch up 'at hat, misteh?"

And the morning customer stepped down to be brushed. Pink swung the long and supple broom in fancy curves and beat out fancy time. As the morning customer started toward the door, Pink whispered, "Gawge Lippincott do n' know 'iss guhl at all, an' I'm sutny goin' 'o keep huh undeh coveh."

On the Relative Value of Education and Wealth

On a bright spring morning, when Pink should have been dwelling on the birth of seasons, he admitted that he was pondering on the benefits of education. Before he spoke, the morning customer noticed that his eyelids were strained, and he whispered to himself.

He worked in silence for several minutes and then consulted the oracle.

"Misteh, I want to ask you q'estion, 'cuz I know you'll tell me right. It's 'bout which is betteh faw you — ej'cation o' money?"

"What got you started on that question?" asked the morning customer.

"Yes, seh, 'ey had a meetin' at 'e F'ed'ick Douglass Club last ev'nin', an' I went 'ith Gawge Lippincott. 'At's 'e q'estion 'ey discussed 'bout, which is betteh faw you to have — ej'cation o' money?"

"Which side did you take?"

"I jus' set theah an' listened to some of 'em hot boys th'ow lang'age at each otheh. 'Ey sutny wuz usin' wuhds 'at neveh'd been used befo'. I guess it was pooh, too. Goodness! 'At Gawge Lippincott jus' spread his wings an' sail 'round an' 'round 'at room like eagle. He neveh touch flooh at all. You talk 'bout me bein' in 'at ahgament! W'y, misteh, I could jus' flutteh a little. I sutny couldn' fly."

"Which side did your friend, Mr. Lippincott, take?"

"Misteh, he couldn' see nothin' but ej'cation. He said 'at a wise boy could make good even if he didn' have 'e coin, but if you had all 'e money you could cah'y an' wuz igno'ant, 'en people wouldn' show no manneh o' respec' faw you."

"Yes, but suppose a man has plenty of money — he can travel around the world and employ people to instruct him, and in a little while he will have an education."

"'At's so, misteh," said Pink, reflectively. 'At's ev'y wuhd so, suah 'nough."

"But, on the other hand," said the morning customer, "suppose that a man has education, but no money, to begin with. Can't he use his education to make money?"

"'At's what he can do," said Pink, solemnly.

"Suppose he makes money and loses it. He still has his education left, has n't he?"

"Misteh, you sutny siftin' it. Yes, seh, you sutny gettin' 'at subjec' right up in 'e cawneh so's it can't get away f'om you."

"You follow my line of reasoning, do you?"

"Go on, misteh, I'm close behind. You can't lose me."

"I say, suppose the educated man loses his money. He still has his education left. But if a man has n't got anything at all but money, and he loses that, where is he? Tell me that."

"Wheah is he? Wheah is he, misteh? W'y, 'at's his finish, suah. My goodness, misteh, I do wish you'd been out to 'at F'ed'ick Douglass Club las' night jus' to toss some of 'at kind o' lang'age at some of 'em cullud bladdehs. Ol' Hahvey Wilson 'uz takin' 'e money side, an' he sutny made mo' noise an' done less talkin' an' any man I eveh see. You neveh know what Hahvey's wantin' to tell you, 'cuz he use 'em wuhds 'at he makes up himself — all 'e time sayin' someping 'bout 'e 'scrambation of illipsical' o' 'ambification faw scientific tomolgy, an' all 'at. He do n' know what 'at means any mo' an you du."

"Well, you know what 'tomology' means, do n't you?" asked the morning customer.

"How's 'at, misteh? 'Tomology'?"

"Yes, the word 'tomology,' you just used. You know what that means, do n't you?"

Pink rubbed the shoe slowly and appeared to be in deep thought.

"I une'stand in gen'al way e' definition, but I can't hahdly tell it."

"'Tomology' means the science of tomatoes."

"Yes, seh. I know it 'uz someping like 'at, but Hahvey Wilson, he didn' know, misteh. He jus' huhd somebody use 'at wuhd, an' he say, ''At's a good wuhd. I jus' need 'at!' Yes, seh, he thinks 'at 'tomology' someping about 'e Bible."

"Well, which side won the debate?"

"Misteh, 'at Gawge Lippincott beat Hahvey Wilson at ev'y tuhn in 'e road. My goodness, he had ol' Hahvey hangin' on 'e ropes, but 'ey done him duht, suah. Hahvey got 'at decision. Ycs, seh; his brotheh-in-law 'uz one of 'e judges, an' 'notheh judge 'uz Lou Pahkeh 'at Gawge kep' out o' bein' janitah at 'e police station. Ol' Gawge sutny had no chance 'genst 'at push."

"Are you a member of the club?"

"No, seh; I jus' kind o' follow ol' Gawge in. 'Bout month ago, misteh, 'ey sutny had a wahm session 'bout 'Which is 'e greates', wateh o' fiah?' I s'pose ol' Gawge did n' say a wuhd 'at night. He jus' ask 'em one q'estion, misteh, 'at settled 'e whole thing. He jus' say, 'Wateh can put out fiah, but how 'bout fiah puttin' out wateh?' Afteh he showed 'at wateh 'uz strongeh 'n fiah, he say, 'What's 'e mos' hahm fiah eveh done?' 'At 'uz 'e Chicago fiah. It jus' buhn up one town, but did n't e' flood wash away ev'ything? W'y, misteh, 'at flood wash away hund'ehds towns 'e size o' Chicago, an' nobody eveh heah anything mo' 'bout 'em."

"Do you believe that story about Noah's ark and the flood?"

"How's 'at, misteh? Do I believe 'at sto'y? Ain' t it wrote down in 'e Bible, huh?"

"Yes, but I did n't know whether you believed it or not."

"Look heah, man! S'pose I did have some doubts 'bout 'at sto'y. Do n't you think I'm eveh foolish 'nough to say so. No, seh; I'm takin' no chances. I jus' say I b'lieve ev'ything 'at's put down an' 'en I'm safe."

"Why, it's just as bad to have a doubt in your mind as it is to come right out and say so," remarked Mr. Clifford, the head barber, who had lounged over to hear the talk.

"No, seh!" replied Pink, emphatically. "'Ey can't prove nothin' 'genst me if I do n't come out an' say someping. S'pose 'ey say, 'Misteh Mahsh, did you al'uz believe 'e Bible?' an' I say, 'Yes, seh.' 'Ey couldn' prove what been in my mind; no, seh. Ain' 'at so, misteh?"

"I'm in doubt about that," said the morning customer.

"But if 'ey say, 'How 'bout 'at mawnin' in 'e bahbeh-shop when you told 'em gem'men 'at you wuz nt' suah 'bout Noah an' 'e ahk?'"

— what could I answeh back? No, seh; you do n't get me into no trouble about 'e Bible. I do n' know what all's in 'at Bible, but I say it's so, o' else it would n't be in. I'm takin' no chances, misteh. I ain' no good chuhch membeh now, but I'm goin' o' keep good on believin' in 'at Bible, so if eveh I get sick o' anything 'e matteh 'ith me, I wont have to squaih myse'f ve'y much. 'At's goin' 'o count faw me, misteh, if I can say I b'lieve 'at Bible all 'e time."

"You have it all figured out," said the morning customer, "and I do n't see how they can lose you."

Pink was much elated to think that he had not been trapped into expressing any doubt as to scriptural revelation.

On the Sin of Neglecting an Opportunity

The friendship between the morning customer and Pink lasted well, because it was never allowed to drift into familiarity. Whenever the morning customer climbed to the throne, he was greeted with formal politeness. He listened gravely when Pink told his secrets, and, by fine tact, invited confidence even while repelling intimacy. He seldom spoke of himself, and there never can be a real companionship between two persons until they have compared experiences.

After the months had passed, Pink knew the morning customer as an exalted and dignified personage who had command of the wisdom of all ages and allowed his light to shine. And that was all he knew.

The morning customer, on the other hand, knew Pink's biography — the boy's early life in an Ohio town, how he followed the race horses to Chicago, why he gave up working in a dairy lunchroom, and so on, up to the time when he took the room at Mrs. Willard's house and was placed in charge of the boot-polishing department in Mr. Clifford's shop.

It has already appeared that he learned of Pink's habits, his falling from grace, and his recovery of the high intentions to be important and have money of his own. With each visit the morning customer learned something more regarding the boy. For instance, one morning the conversation turned upon the subject of dramatic art, and Pink gave the opinion that "Camille" was the greatest play ever written.

"Took a guhl to see 'at 'Camille' one night," he said. "She jus' shiveh an' hang on to me all 'e way home. I got puhty well roused myse'f."

At another time, soon after Pink had expressed his entire faith in the Bible (as set forth in the preceding chapter), he talked of music, and said that "rag-time" melodies pleased him, but that he dared not listen to them during business hours, because the mists came before his eyes and he became so excited that he could not shine shoes. He told of his belief that the angels in heaven played "rag-time" music, and he regarded this as an inducement for all colored people to lead pure lives.

While they were talking of "rag-time" music, the morning customer asked why it was that a colored man could dance so much better than a white man. Pink advanced the explanation that the colored man had fewer bones than the white man, and had his joints peculiarly constructed, according to an all-wise plan. He also held that the white men's bones were "brickle," while the colored man could bend his frame and assume certain shapes which added to the charm of his performance as a dancer. The morning customer shook his head in doubt, and Pink said that a doctor had once explained to him the construction of a colored man, telling him, among other things, that the skull was an inch thick and that the only tender part of the anatomy was the shin-bone.

It happened that just after Pink had won his point concerning the bony structure of the members of his race, two barbers and a man in the second chair became involved in loud talk about the continuous war-cloud in Europe. This interruption gave the morning customer a chance to retire gracefully from the dispute as to anatomy, so he asked:

"Have you been reading the war news in the papers?"

"Misteh, I got no time faw 'at wah when 'ey 's fo' tracks runnin'; no, seh. I been too busy watchin' 'em at Memphis to know 'bout 'at wah. I mahked 'em yes'day, misteh, an' three out o' fo' win, an' I didn' have a cent on one of 'em."

"I understand. You've been making these mind bets — figuring how much you might have won."

"Misteh, I ought to be cah'yin' roll to-day 'at'd look like bolt o' wall-papeh. "Yes, seh, I had ol' Domingo at Memphis, an' 'at Pahson at Newpoht. Cullud boy tol' me to be suah an' get someping on Pahson as soon as he 'uz good odds. Yes'day, misteh, he 'uz six to one, an' I know he couldn' lose, an' heah I set rubbing up tans faw nasty ol' ten a throw when I ought to been oveh in' at back room playin' my cloze on 'at Pahson. W'y misteh, he went past 'em jus like 'ey was tied. I know wheah I could got five dollahs yes'day, too. I take 'at five and play Domingo an' Pahson, an' I get mo' 'an hund'ehd of 'em big smiling dollahs to-day."

"I'm afraid I'll never cure you of gambling."

"W'y, misteh, when you see on 'e blackboahd 'at Pahson's six to one, an' you know he can't lose, I'm tellin' you, misteh, it ain' right to keep 'at money in yo' pocket. If 'at bookmakeh say, 'Come an' take my money,' yo' sutny foolish if you do n' do it."

"I can't see that you've ruined very many bookmakers. Where's all the money you've won on the races?"

"Hush, man! I do n' s'pose I done a thing to ol' Sly Libson one day, did I? I jus' caught 'at rascal seven to one, an' I come back f'om 'e pahk in open caih'age smokin' one of 'em pooh fifteen-cent cigahs."

"Yes, you told me about that. You went out that night and lost your job. How long did your money last you?"

"Neveh mind 'bout 'at time, misteh. Nex' time Misteh Mahsh gets on one of 'em good things, he's goin' 'o take 'at money an' plant it deep, suah."

"What! Are you going to save money at last?"

"'At's what I need, misteh. 'At's what I got to have."

"Well, that's a virtuous resolution, certainly, but I do n't think you'll ever make any money playing the races."

"You can't tell, misteh. I been feelin' ve'y lucky for sev'al days."

"Well, I hope you'll not be disappointed. Since when have you had this desire to save money?"

"Well, misteh, you got to have a little, o' they sutny got no use faw you."

"Who has n't any use for you? I wonder if you are contemplating matrimony."

"Hush, man!"

"What's her name — the new one?"

"Who? 'At Miss Belle Hopkins? I neveh say I 'uz goin' 'o join up 'ith 'at lady."

"No, but I'm very suspicious."

Pink laughed away down in his throat, and shook his head warningly. "I do n' say I will mah'y 'at lady, an' I do n' say I won't do it. She's a cana'y buhd, misteh, an' she sings sweet song, but 'e cullud boy ain' got no cage. You can't neveh live on 'em cake-walks. Cake-walks is good, misteh, but you can't eat 'em, no seh! 'At's ev'y wuhd so. Thank you, seh. How's 'at, misteh? Keep 'e change? Oh, I s'pose I do n' know how, do I? I tol' you, misteh, 'at I wuz feelin' lucky."

On Secret Defamation of Character

There was a dark cloud in the sky.

Pink Marsh told the morning customer about it at the first opportunity. He began by saying that he would have to write another letter.

"What's the matter?" asked the morning customer.

"Dahk cloud in 'e sky, misteh. Yes, seh, 'ey 's a dahk cloud in 'e sky, caused by some low-down cullud pusson, who I call a snake-in-'e-grass right to his ve'y face."

"Who is the snake-in-the-grass?"

"'At's what I can't find out, misteh."

"Well, how can you tell him anything to his face, then?"

"Jus' le' me know who it is, misteh; 'at 's all Misteh Mahsh caihs to know. Yes, seh, he be layin' in 'at shiny box 'an people go by an' say: 'Jus' looks like he's 'sleep, do n't he?' Co'se, his cloze goin' 'o coveh up all 'em holes I cahve in him. I'm goin' 'o leave 'nough o' him to make a good fune'al, at' 'at 's 'bout all."

"It is n't George this time — George, what's his name?"

"No, seh, it ain't Gawge. I can't find out who done it, but if I look in ev'y house on Deahbohn St'eet, I'm suah to find him some time o' otheh, an' when I do — hush man! You jus' listen on 'e Nawth Side, an' you heah him squawk out Twent'-Sevem Street. Yes, seh, yo' next."

The last was addressed to a young man in checked clothes, who had edged up and was listening with a steadfast grin.

"Who's that you're goin' to do up?" he asked.

"'At's nobody, misteh," replied Pink, with an averted wink at the morning customer. "I wouldn' huht nobody. You jus' have a good chaih, misteh, an' I'll sutny use you right in ve'y few minutes. Heah's mawnin' papeh, seh, 'at's got all 'bout 'at Cong'ess. Yes, seh, you get oveh by 'e window yo' suah to get plenty o' light. Yes, seh, I'll be ready faw you, seh, in ve'y shawt time."

Pink diplomatically steered the young man over to the window and supplied him with the remnant of a morning paper, after which he returned to the morning customer, with a sidewise expression of satisfied cunning.

"I do n' wan' no sody-juggleh out o' no drug-stoah to stan' round an' rubbeh when I'm talkin' 'em p'ivate mattehs," he said, confidentially, as he resumed his place on the stool. "I got to use him propeh, 'cuz his money goes on 'e street-cahs jus' same as yo's, but I sutny do n' want to be conf'dential 'ith no boy 'at tosses 'em aig phosphates."

"Well, what's the purport of all this sanguinary conversation?" asked the morning customer, who had noted that Pink always mapped out the vengeance first and told of the provocation afterward.

Pink smiled in upward admiration, and then his shoulders shook in rapid measure, showing that he was enjoying himself inwardly.

"Ev'y day new ones, misteh!" he exclaimed. "Ev'y day new ones! Some hulleh 'an othehs, but all of 'em too wahm faw pooh cullud boy."

"Did n't I understand you to say that you were going to slaughter some one?"

"Misteh, heah's what I'm goin' 'o do: I'm goin' 'o cut my name in 'at cullud rascal so deep 'at you can read it f'om behind same as in front. I'm goin' 'o stand him up an' whittle him. Yes, seh; I'm goin' 'o take off so much o' his weight 'at he'll be in new class. I'll sutny trim him good. When I finish 'ith him an' pack my tools, he'll be diff'ent shape — 'at's a fac'."

"I think I begin to understand," said the morning customer. "Somebody has stolen that new girl."

"Who? Who? Do n' neveh believe it, seh. No, seh! If 'ey get 'at lady 'way f'om William Pinckney, 'ey sutny got to pull 'uh. She could n' leave me if she want' to. You know what she say? 'Misteh Mahsh, 'ey 's one floweh 'at blooms in ev'y gahden, an' you ah my honeysuckle.'"

"That's very pretty."

"It ain't ev'y dahk-haihed boy 'at gets 'at kind, misteh."

"I suppose not. Well, if you have n't lost Miss Hopkins, what seems to be the trouble?"

"Yes, seh, 'e trouble is, misteh, 'at some cullud pusson's out to poison my cha'cteh. Somebody's been knockin' me 'ith ol' Mis' Hopkins. Goodness, misteh! She tell Belle 'at she heah I like gin an' roll 'e bones an' play numbehs an' cah'y razah, an' — "

"And steal chickens?"

"Suah! Wuhse kind o' chicken-lifteh — steal 'em in front o' butcheh-shops an' stoahs — steal 'ese 'at's picked an' cleaned. Yes, seh, whoeveh it is 'at's knockin', I s'pose, got me down faw stealin' dead chickens. It takes a spoht to go afteh a live chicken, misteh, but when you take dead one, 'at's jus' plain stealin'. I s'pose I'm dead-chicken thief."

"Somebody's been telling all these things to Miss Hopkins's mother — is that it?"

"Misteh, I ought to be oveh in 'e jail, an' have my pickchah in 'e papeh. Neveh mind, misteh, I'm waitin'."

"Do you suspect any one?"

"I'll tell you 'bout 'at, misteh. Miss Belle got a cousin, Chesteh Hopkins, 'at leads 'e singin' at e' chuhch. Chesteh got side-whiskehs. Look out faw one 'ith side-whiskehs, misteh! It wuz n' neveh meant faw no cullud pusson to have side-whiskehs. Chesteh got a ve'y wahm set of 'em, too. An' he weahs eyeglasses! Hush! I tell you, misteh, he ain't right. He do n' look like no cullud pusson. He look mo' like some Sunday-school white man 'at jus' shift his cullah. I guess he ain' no cullud man, neetheh, come to think 'bout it. Chesteh wuz 'e fus' Af'o-Ameh'can on Deahbohn Street. He's suah 'nough Af'o-Ameh'can, an' he got a bad eye in his head faw Misteh William Pinckney Mahsh. Him an' Brotheh Fehguson, 'e preacheh, jus' about own 'at chuhch at ol' Mis' Hopkins goes to, an' I do n' s'pose ol' Chesteh goin' o' ovehlook no chance to spoil my bets. 'Cose I ain' been goin' to chuhch ve'y often in 'e las' twenty yeahs o' so, an' mebbe Chesteh do n' think I got no ticket faw to swing on 'e sweet cha'iot," and Pink laughed.

"Have n't been to church, and you're proud of it," said the morning customer, shaking his head. "I'm afraid you're a hopeless case."

"I been sev'al times lately 'ith Miss Belle."

"Trying to get on good terms with Mrs. Hopkins."

"I s'pose 'at's a bad guess, misteh. Anyways I ain't win 'at ol' lady yet. Goodness, misteh! I like to know who feed huh 'at mean talk 'bout me. Somebody scandalize my name, suah. On'y one thing squaih me 'ith Mis' Hopkins — 'at's one of 'em lettehs. Make me good one, misteh, an' put in some sc'ipchah. Ain't scaihed o' losin' my baby, but I want to be so good up at 'e Hopkins house 'at a good wahm dinneh be waitin' faw me any time I call."

The morning customer promised.

On Conjuration

The morning customer spent fifteen minutes in composing the letter which was to give Pink Marsh a sure standing with Belle Hopkins's mother. He pushed aside the letter waiting to be answered, and devoted himself to the labor of love. Was he prompted by the hopes of a reward? None — except that reward which comes to the unselfish man when he knows that he has helped to complicate a love affair.

He took it to Mr. Clifford's shop two days after his promise had been given. Pink was anxious to hear the letter, and he exercised great haste in shining a pair of scaly gaiters, so that he could go into a close session with the morning customer.

"Got 'at, misteh?" he asked, cautiously.

"Which? O, that letter? Yes, I dashed off a few lines and had them typewritten. I've left it so that you can sign your name at the bottom — that is, if it suits you."

"Suit me, misteh? I know it's good befo' you read it."

"I did n't know Mrs. Hopkins's first name, so I left that blank. Do you know it?"

"No, seh, I do n't. Jus' Mis' Hopkins; 'at's all we eveh call huh."

"Has she got a husband?"

"Yes, seh, she got a husband."

"What's his name?"

"Zig Lucas."

"Her name is Mrs. Hopkins and her husband's name is Zig Lucas — how do you make that out?"

"Mis' Hopkins, she been mah'ied befo'. I guess so wuz ol' Zig. He got boy Spotswood Lucas', 'at ain' no kin to Belle at all. Ol' Spot neveh done day's wuhk in his life. Sick all 'e time. Yes, seh, too sick to wuhk — just able to eat an' play pool."

A LABOR OF LOVE

"I put it 'Mrs. Hopkins' here. We'll let it go at that. Are you ready to hear it?"

"Yes, seh, misteh. Do n' make it too loud."

"'Mrs. Hopkins — My Dear Madam: It is with —'"

"Hold on, mistch. You want to get me in trouble 'ith 'at ol' Zig? What you got me sayin' to Mis' Hopkins?"

"Why, you address her as 'My dear madam.'"

"Ain't 'at puhty wahm to give 'at ol' guhl? When she reads 'at, she think I'm afteh huh, 'stead o' Belle. 'Deah madam' — my goodness! 'At's lovin' talk, suah."

"O, that does n't mean anything. Any letter to a married lady of your acquaintance should begin that way. You leave it alone. That will please her."

He read the letter:

"MRS. HOPKINS — My Dear Madam: It is with feelings of indiscriminate respect that I address you upon a subject which I regard as altogether behooving.

"'Be thou as chaste as ice, as pure as snow,
Thou shall not escape calumny.'

"How true this is! It is with excruciating surprise that I learn of a recent attempt to cast aspersions on my character, which I have always sought to keep herbiverous. As you are doubtless cognizant, I have lately endeavored to place myself in immediate juxtaposition to your daughter, Belle, whose caloric properties are such as to excite my profound admiration. At present she is the most salubrious object within my range of vision. Animated, no doubt, by the rancor of envy, some inconsequential marplot is striving to elucidate my superiority. I wish to deny emphatically anything you may hear which is not derogatory to my character. Without going into details, I may say with all the vehemence of asseveration, that I am the most superior Afro-American who ever approached on the rural highway. This epistle will doubtless remove all eccentricities from your mind, and make you disposed to regard me as the proper recipient of gustatory favors. Thanking you for your kind attention, I am, with sufficient respect, yours truly."

While the letter was being read, Pink emitted tremulous groans, and at the conclusion he said, in an awed whisper: "O, man! O, man! O, man!"

"I did n't think it was best to deny, specifically, any of the charges against you," said the morning customer. "I simply put in a general plea and threw you on the mercy of the court. Have you any changes to suggest?"

"Look heah, misteh, why do n't you ask me to go out an' change e' stahs in 'e sky? No, seh; 'at letteh's too good faw any boy my ej'cation to trifle 'ith it. When Mis' Hopkins read 'at, she'll know I'm good. I can jus' see myse'f eatin' Sunday hinneh up at 'at house.'"

"You've never eaten up there yet, eh?"

"I do n' daih to, misteh; no, seh."

"Why not?"

"I'm 'fraid of 'at ol' guhl. She's f'om Kentucky, an' she knows too much. I'm 'fraid she' cunjuh me, suah."

"Conjure you? What does that mean?"

"Hush, misteh, you know what 'at means betteh 'an I do — a man yo' ej'cation."

"I assure you that I do n't know. How could Mrs. Hopkins conjure you?"

"Well, misteh, I do n' hahdly b'lieve it myse'f, but I heah them Southehn cullud people tell 'bout puttin' 'at stuff in yo' eatin', an' it make someping grow inside o' you — someping like lizahd."

"O, pshaw! You do n't believe all that stuff, do you?"

"Look heah, misteh man, some of 'em ol' cullud people 'at's lived down South can use you bad if you ain' caihful. Bud Law'ence tol' me he saw man in Kentucky 'at got cunjuhed by an ol' cullud lady, an' he had to sen' to Loueyville faw ol' cullud doctah. Doctah come an' dig all 'em roots an' 'uhbs an' make tea faw 'at cullud man, an' he toss up two white lizahds. 'At's what Bud seen 'ith his own eyes."

"How did these lizards get into him?"

"My goodness! He got cunjuhed, misteh — at's how he got 'em. He had fuss 'ih an ol' cullud lady, an' she put 'at cunjuh stuff in his dinneh. Yes, seh, you can laugh, misteh, but 'ey's sutny someping in 'at cunjuh business. Look heah, seh, did n' you eveh put hoss-haih into bottle an' see it tuhn into snake? Yes, seh, I seen 'at myse'f. 'At's what 'em cunjuh people do — put someping like 'at into yo' victuals, an' it get inside o' you, an' you begin feelin' bad an' get thinneh an' thinneh, an if you do n' get 'at boy out o' you — goin' 'o have a black beh'yin, suah. Yes, seh, em cunjuh people come an' plant someping in front o' yo' house, too. You walk oveh it ev'y day, an' afteh while you get sick, an' fus' thing you know you jus' tuhn up yo' toes. I do n' want nothin' to do 'ith 'em cunjuh people."

"Well, do you think Mrs. Hopkins has the power to conjure you?"

"Yes, seh, most any o' em ol' cullud ladies f'om 'e South got 'at poweh. Ol' Pink sutny ain' goin' 'o eat no dinneh in 'at house 'til he knows 'at Mis' Hopkins likes him. She's been talkin' bad 'bout me, an' I go to 'at house an' eat — you do n' know what she do to me!"

"Have n't you got your rabbit's foot?"

"Yes, seh, you can laugh, misteh, but do n't you fool yo' se'f 'bout 'at cunjuh'n. Someping in it, suah."

Pink shook his head solemnly, and appeared to be somewhat grieved that the morning customer went away laughing.

On the Doubts which Precede Matrimony

Pink Marsh reported to the morning customer that the letter to Mrs. Hopkins had accomplished its purpose.

"She ain't th'ough lookin' oveh 'at letter yet," he said, shaking his head and bubbling with laughter. "Ol Zig, he did n' eveh b'lieve I wrote it. He tell Belle to ask me who wrote 'at letteh. I say, 'Look it oveh, guhl, an' see whose name's down at 'e bottom.' My goodness, misteh! 'At letteh did suit ol' Mis' Hopkins! She likes 'em hot wuhds, just 'e kind you put in 'at letteh. Yes, seh, when Brotheh Fehguson up at 'e chuhch begin to toss 'em hot wuhds at 'e brethe'n an' sistuhn, 'at's when ol' Mis' Hopkins begin to get happy an' let go."

"You do n't think she'll conjure you now?"

"Cunjuh me, misteh? Pink is huh honey-boy now — suah! She likes me now, 'cuz she find out I got wahm ej'cation. All 'at talk 'bout 'medimate justamisition —'"

"'Immediate juxtaposition'?"

"Yes, seh; at's what win ol' Mis' Hopkins. She's sutny usin' me good 'ese days. 'Misteh Mahsh, I hope yo' feelin' ambulous 'iss ev'nin'. 'O yes, Mis' Hopkins, I'm ve'y lansimous."

"You did n't tell her you were lansimous, did you?"

"W'y — yes seh. I jus' say like 'at, 'I'm feelin' ratheh lansimous.'"

"'Lansimous' means that you are suffering from remorse — that you've got something on your mind."

"Yes, seh; 'at's so, misteh; but Mis' Hopkins she did n't know what 'at meant. I s'pose she thought I jus' meant I wuz feelin' well."

"So you're welcome to the house now?"

"Hush, man! Las' night an' night befo'. Settin' on 'e front steps 'ith my sweet thing, an' holdin' on to huh so she would n' get lost. O, I guess she's pooh," and Pink hit the box with his polishing-brush and laughed immoderately.

"BUD"

"Well, if Mrs. Hopkins is won over and Belle loves you, I do n't see that there is anything to prevent an early union."

"You mean faw us to get mah'ied?"

"Why, certainly. You've been courting this girl for several weeks, have n't you? You say she loves you, and, according to your own admission, you have visited her at her home and sat on the front steps with her — probably embraced her."

Pink was bent over the shoe, quivering with laughter at the recital.

"I have helped you to win the favor of the young lady's mother," continued the morning customer. "Now that the girl and her mother trust you, are you going to betray that trust? You talk as if you did n't intend to marry her at all."

"Look heah, mistch," said Pink, still bubbling with laughter, "what you think we goin' 'o live on — buck dances? In 'e fus' place, 'at maih'age license cost two dollahs. I ain't even got nasty ol' two, no, seh! How 'bout 'em lace cuhtains faw windows, an' pohk-chops to eat ev'y mawning'? Huh-uh! Can't get mah'ied till I got 'at roll."

"About the first time I ever came into this shop, six months ago, I advised you to begin saving your money. If you had started in and saved two dollars a week, you would have had fifty or sixty dollars by this time. With that much you could have bought a new suit of clothes, rented a house and made a first payment on some furniture. As it is, how much have you this morning?"

"Misteh, if 'ey had n't rung in hosses on me las' night, I'd have sev'al dollahs 'iss mawnin'."

"So you've been playing craps again? That was after your call on Miss Hopkins, I presume."

"Yes, seh; I had 'em comin' good, but little Joe use me bad, an' somebody get in hosses, an' 'en a big cullud fellow 'at drives caih'age jus' took me 'way in his cloze. Ol' Gawge Lippincott went broke, too."

"Well, there you are again — gambling? Does this girl know that you gamble?"

"She do n' caih how much I gamble, if I on'y pull out someping. Co'se she got no use faw man 'at's cleaned all 'e time. You got to flash two-bit piece once in awhile to keep 'em smilin'."

"Well, what will be the outcome of this affair with Miss Hopkins? If you do n't intend to marry her, why have you pursued her?"

"Look heah, misteh, I do n' say I won't mah'y 'at Miss Belle Hopkins. I s'pose I might if I had mo' money; but you know what I say to you head one day — cake-walks is good, but you sutny can't eat 'em. If I jus' get on good live one some time, 'bout fawty to one, an' play five dollahs — hush, misteh! We be livin' in one of 'em white houses 'ith blue cuhtains in 'e windows, an' all 'em red velvet sofys an' chaihs, wall-papeh coveh'd 'ith mawnin'-glo'ies, Brussel cahpet on 'e flooh —"

"Picture of Peter Jackson in the parlor," suggested the morning customer.

Pink yawped at the idea, and leaned forward on the box in a convulsion of mirth.

"Misteh, yo' sutny good! Yes, seh; we got to have ol' Peteh. My goodness! 'At's fine house I got, suah! I can jus' see myse'f settin' in 'at house eatin' chicken 'ith home gravy — betteh'n any of 'iss heah rest'ant gravy, too! Home gravy an' sweet potatoes! My goodness! I jus' lingeh 'round 'e table an' make trouble faw 'at kind o' eatin,' I s'pose. I guess I jus' hate 'at home gravy. Um-m-m-m! It's ba-ad!"

By this time Pink was talking to himself and wagging his head gravely. The morning customer interrupted the soliloquy, and said "Im afraid you'll never realize your expectations, unless you stop playing craps."

"Some day I'll get 'em goin', an' I'll have all 'e money on 'e South Side. Yes, seh; 'Keep on a-tryin', brotheh,' 'at's jus' what Preacheh Fehguson says. You'll see, misteh. I jus' feel 'at I got money comin' to me."

The morning customer went away, leaving Pink cheered and uplifted by the abiding pleasures of hope.

On Doing the Best One Can

"He come in here yesterday smokin' a big cigar and all dressed up in his best clothes, and said he'd quit — said he had something better."

Mr. Clifford was speaking. The morning customer stood in hesitancy, looking at the half-grown colored youth who sat on Pink's stool in the corner, humped above a patent-leather shoe which had the shape of a sword-fish.

"You do n't know where he went?" asked the morning customer.

"No, and I do n't care. I won't have him around here again. This new boy's all right. He'll give you a good shine."

Mr. Clifford evidently believed that the morning customer had been coming into the place to have his shoes shined!

The morning customer murmured a falsehood to the effect that he might "come in later," and then he retreated, before Mr. Clifford could say anything more in favor of the new boy.

That was his last visit to the shop. He rather expected to receive a communication from Pink, but no postal-card came, and, to tell the truth, after a few days had passed, he gave no further thought to the "lansimous" boy and his quest for a "baby."

In a busy town, such as Chicago, experiences crowd upon one another, and every live man of the morning-customer kind is so intent on making his fortune that he has little time to tilt back and wonder what has become of the friends of yesterday. Within a month after the disappearance, the season of helpful talks with Pink became ancient history. The morning customer hurried past Mr. Clifford's shop day after day, without seeing it or knowing of its existence. He would be whispering to himself the terms of a contract, or squinting through his glasses to see into the plans of those who wanted to keep him away from his fortune. To such a man, buildings fuse into one another as they slide by in panorama, and pedestrians are so many things to be dodged. The morning customer raced every day. He went to a "parlor" to have his shoes cleaned. Twelve white boys in blue jackets leaned over in a row and worked at high speed. They seldom spoke to the men in the chairs, who regarded one another with fretful suspicion, and turned their morning papers over and over and inside out.

It would be satisfying to know that the morning customer often smiled at recollection of what Pink had told him, and wondered if the boy had saved any money.

He had not the time. That is the fact of the matter. He was jumping with elevators, a hundred feet at an upward leap; racing to court-rooms, where he messed papers and whispered with hollow-eyed accomplices; and sometimes he went out of town on night trains, so as to avoid the deadly sin of traveling during business hours.

One night he boarded a train at a suburban crossing. The train was bound for Kansas City. In the sleeping-car the berths were "made up." He went along the narrow aisle between the stuffy curtains to where a porter with a white coat was whispering to some hidden passenger. He nudged the porter from behind.

"My goodness, misteh!"

It was Pink.

"Any lowers left?" asked the morning customer, closing his teeth together in the endeavor to keep a serious face.

"Well, my goodness, misteh. Well, seh, it's you, suah! My goodness! I'm sutny glad to see you once mo'. I declaih!"

"I did n't expect to see *you*, Pink. Have you a lower berth?"

"Misteh, if I did n' have none, I'd jus' tuhn somebody out an' let you have it. My goodness! Well! Well!"

"Where's the conductor?"

"Yes, seh, he's in 'e cah ahead, seh."

"Well, I'll sit in the smoking-room a while."

He went into the smoking compartment and lighted a cigar. A short man with jewelry and a silk cap had been holding the compartment alone. He looked up, as if in annoyance, when the morning customer came in, and then threw away his cigar and rocked away to bed.

The morning customer sprawled out on the plush cushion and smoked. He grinned around his cigar, and once or twice he laughed aloud. Presently Pink slipped in and sat on a low stool. He looked steadfastly at the morning customer for many seconds, his eyes rolled sidewise, and then he burst into laughter.

"Well, my goodness!" he said.

"You're a real porter, now."

"Me an' Misteh Pullman's 'e real boys, suah. No mo' settin' round 'ith 'em white barbehs. Huh-uh!"

He paused and looked at the morning customer in blissful silence, and then gave another bellow of laughter, so that he had to restrain himself by putting one hand over his mouth.

"What's the matter with you, anyway?" asked the morning customer, leaning forward so as to make himself heard above the pounding of the train.

"Misteh, someping happen to me since I seen you."

"What was it?"

"Make a guess, misteh," and he was still laughing.

"I know, all right. Did you go and do it?"

"Look out, misteh! Do n't ask! Ol' Mistch Mahsh mah'ied man."

The morning customer smiled benevolently. "Glad to hear it," said he. "What was her name — Belle?"

"Who? 'At Belle Hopkins? No, seh! Huh-uh! I did n' mah'y 'at guhl."

"You did n't?"

"Look heah, misteh! Crep' up to 'at house one night an' ketch new cullud boy 'ith both ahms 'round 'at guhl. I jus' say, 'Good-by, my honey!' Yes, seh, she lose Misteh Mahsh. Got someping betteh 'n 'at Belle. Got lady 'at had p'opehty. Go 'way! I s'pose I do n' know thing!"

"Got property, eh?"

"Yes, seh — widow."

"A widow!"

"No mo' room-rents, misteh. I jus' look oveh 'at Mis' White's house an' say, 'O, I guess 'iss'll do me.' I had huh lovin' me befo' she know me two days. I went faw 'at lady an' I landed 'uh."

"How long have you been married?"

"Mo' 'an a month."

"Is she a young woman?"

"She ain't young as some of 'em other babies I had lookin' out faw me, but you 'membeh what I tol' you once, misteh? Cake-walks is good, but you can't eat 'em. You do n' ketch me stahvin'. No, seh! 'At lady I got ain't so wahm on cloze as some of 'em, but she sutny fix up a pohk chop 'at's bad to eat. 'At love's all right, misteh; but Misteh Mahsh sutny got to have his pohk chops."

"Well, are you saving any money?"

"Look heah! Fannie takes 'at money 'way f'om me an' just gives me 'nough to live on. My goodness, misteh! I sutny got to hold out on Fannie when I play 'em numbehs."

"Have you caught anything yet?"

"No, seh; but I come might' neah it las' week. Got two of 'em — want fawty-eight, an' fawty-sevem come."

"What became of the other girl — Belle?"

"Do n' ask me, misteh! She's nothin to me — no, seh. Huh an 'at Lo'ena Jackson — look heah! I'll have one of 'em guhls hiahed to wuhk 'round 'e house an' help Fannie."

"I thought you were going to marry Belle."

"No, seh, I neveh caih faw 'at guhl noways. I done betteh! My goodness, misteh! I s'pose I'm pooh. Got my own dooh-step to set on, new suit o' cloze, joined 'e lodge. Do n' speak to 'em cheap cullud people no mo'. Goin' 'o tuhn in, seh? Jus' you put 'em shoes outside an' I'll give 'em one of 'em ol' shines like you use' to get."

The morning customer rolled into a lower berth, and lay between the cool sheets, smiling hard at the upper berth, which Pink had lifted out of the way, in violation of a very strict rule. The morning customer paid for a lower berth, and owned a section. He was trying to imagine Pink's house — the wall-paper, the illuminated curtains, the nickeled stove in the front room, and the picture of Abraham Lincoln. He heard creeping foot-falls just outside his berth, and then a voice, "Good-night, seh."